Breen grunted, "Rooftop, tone.

So Longarm said, "I see the smoke. They ahint that false front above the hardware. How bad are you hit?"

The older lawman wheezed, "Bad enough. Go *git* him, pard!"

So Longarm tried and that was easier said than done. He'd had no idea Market Street was really that wide before he'd run across it, zigzagging from side to side, as somewhere ahead of him more shots rang out. And then he was inside a narrow hardware store, befogged with swirling gun smoke. But as he threw down on the only movement ahead of him, it called out, "Don't shoot! I'm with you! Heard the son of a bitch atop my roof. Saw poor Marshal Breen go down across the way. Emptied this new Winchester up through the ceiling. Fifteen rounds without one jam and ain't that something?"

Longarm took a deep breath and said, "Cover me. I got to go up."

The hardware man warned, "If he's still up yonder, and still alive, you're fixing to get your head blown off, mister!"

To which Longarm could only reply, "I ain't a mister. I'm the law. And I never said I *wanted* to go up. I only said I *had* to."

DON'T MISS THESE
ALL-ACTION WESTERN SERIES
FROM THE BERKLEY PUBLISHING GROUP

THE GUNSMITH by J. R. Roberts
Clint Adams was a legend among lawmen, outlaws, and ladies.
They called him . . . the Gunsmith.

LONGARM by Tabor Evans
The popular long-running series about Deputy U.S. Marshal
Long—his life, his loves, his fight for justice.

SLOCUM by Jake Logan
Today's longest-running action Western. John Slocum rides
a deadly trail of hot blood and cold steel.

BUSHWHACKERS by B. J. Lanagan
An action-packed series by the creators of Longarm! The
rousing adventures of the most brutal gang of cutthroats ever
assembled—Quantrill's Raiders.

DIAMONDBACK by Guy Brewer
Dex Yancey is Diamondback, a Southern gentleman turned
con man when his brother cheats him out of the family fortune. Ladies love him. Gamblers hate him. But nobody pulls
one over on Dex . . .

WILDGUN by Jack Hanson
Will Barlow's continuing search for his daughter, kidnapped
by the Blackfeet Indians who slaughtered the rest of his family.

TABOR EVANS

LONGARM

AND THE WIDOW'S SPITE

JOVE BOOKS, NEW YORK

This is a work of fiction. Names, characters, places, and incidents either are the product of the author's imagination or are used fictitiously, and any resemblance to actual persons, living or dead, business establishments, events, or locales is entirely coincidental.

LONGARM AND THE WIDOW'S SPITE

A Jove Book / published by arrangement with
the author

PRINTING HISTORY
Jove edition / November 2001

Visit our website at
www.penguinputnam.com

ISBN: 0-515-13171-7

A JOVE BOOK®
Jove Books are published by The Berkley Publishing Group,
a division of Penguin Putnam Inc.,
375 Hudson Street, New York, New York 10014.
JOVE and the "J" design
are trademarks belonging to Penguin Putnam Inc.

PRINTED IN THE UNITED STATES OF AMERICA

10 9 8 7 6 5 4 3 2 1

Chapter 1

Cracker Marner had ridden hard up the Ogallala Trail, played hard at Fat Edna's house of ill repute and found it awesomely easy to die in the Boxelder Saloon. Things could go that way in Hardwater on a Saturday night during a market drive.

Few who'd known Cracker Marner in life were surprised to hear his luck had run out at last. The handful of kith and kin brave enough to talk to the hard-driving and demon-driven contract drover had tried to warn him there were strangers you could rawhide and there were some it was best not to mess with. But the handsome, husky Texican known as Cracker for three good reasons remained convinced to his last brag in the Boxelder Saloon that he had just about the whole world scared.

He hadn't been too far off. They'd called him Cracker partly because his elders had come west with their scrub stock and drover's whips from the pine woods of Georgia, partly because of the skill with which the professional trail boss cracked the awesome length of braided rawhide he packed in addition to his ivory-gripped and silver inlaid Remington .44-40 and partly because he pistol-whipped anyone but his wife and mother for calling him Courtney, as he'd been sprinkled thirty-seven years and seventy-four days before the late summer evening he'd tried to rawhide the wrong man at one end of the bar in the Boxelder Saloon.

It was later agreed that whoever he might have been, the solitary drinker who'd gunned down the one and original Cracker Marner could not have looked like all that much. Nobody startled by the sudden gunplay in a crowded, dimly lit and already smoke-filled saloon had more than a dim memory of dark, dusty trail duds, a high-crowned, broad-brimmed Stetson shading any features under it and a Colt Lightning carried low in a tied-down, side-draw holster. Such details were more interesting than others when one sized up the others along the bar. So the otherwise inoffensive solitary drinker down to that end of the bar had been left in peace with his own lonesome troubles until Cracker Marner had noticed him there.

Since what had followed had happened so fast, nobody there but the stranger, who nobody could identify, or Cracker Marner, who was dead, would have been able to recall their argument in detail, if *argument* had not been too strong a word for what had happened.

The only witnesses who'd been paying any mind at all had naturally come in just moments before with the jovial bully they rode for. Tiny Fulton, Marner's *segundo* and a whip cracker of some repute in his own right, later denied but might have been heard telling his boss what his dear old dad had once said about that quiet little hombre drinking alone and not bothering anybody. But whatever was said by whomsoever in the few minutes on this earth remaining to Cracker Marner, the trail boss had swaggered over to the smaller dark stranger to declare in the tone of a man who was used to having his own way that

2

his long-lost bastard child with the sissy cap pistol was about to buy him a drink.

The few in the crowd who'd paid enough attention to glance that way agreed the smaller man wearing the bigger hat and that double-action .38 had simply drawn and fired; after that memories tended to disagree in detail.

Those sober enough to later describe toad squat had naturally hit the sawdust-covered floor and stayed down until the last echo of the last round of .38-30 faded away in the uncertain light. By the time most looked up the dimly lit interior of an already smoke-filled saloon was befogged by swirling white clouds of corned black powder smoke as easy to see through as unbaled cotton and as sweet to inhale as the fumes of your average volcano. So nobody there could rightly say just when the stranger might have left or where he might have been headed. All anyone could say for certain was that, as the place calmed down and the smoke slowly cleared, Cracker Marner, alone, was still with them, smiling softly up at the pressed tin ceiling with four powder-burnt holes in the front of his sailcloth shirt spaced tight enough to be covered by one playing card when a gambler present so experimented.

The trail town of Hardwater straddled the Colorado–Kansas line for the same reasons the federally approved Ogallala cattle trail ran string straight, north and south, along that same neutral line that nobody was allowed to straddle with a homestead claim or wire fence. But, seeing the Boxelder Saloon's end of the east-west Market Street lay a few hundred yards inside Colorado jurisdiction, the deputy coroner stuck with the killing convened his inquest across the street in the more seemly lobby of the Majestic Hotel.

Not that it really mattered, much, in the end. Whether the late Courtney a.k.a. Cracker Marner or the unknown

3

and vaguely described dark stranger had started the fight, there was no doubt the quieter man had been way quicker. Everyone agreed that once the smoke had cleared Marner's own gun was still holstered and his big, noisy bull-whip was still lashed in place on his other hip.

None of the few locals present in the Boxelder Saloon at the time had ever seen that nondescript stranger before or since. Those riders who'd been passing through were naturally with their own outfits, mostly from Texas or the somewhat closer Cherokee Strip. To a man they denied knowing that one rider old Cracker never should have messed with. When the deputy coroner wondered aloud whether any Texican Rebel might turn a pal in to North Range law it was Tiny Fulton, the dead man's own *segundo,* who pointed out that there were close to two dozen riders who'd come up the trail with poor old Cracker, there in town and still just as interested as any damn Yankee deputy coroner in seeing justice done.

It was Fulton who first raised the issue of the Marner widows, *two* Marner widows, he had to explain all this bullshit to, once he'd seen the consolidated herd on up to Nebraska loading chutes and the body of old Cracker back to the headwaters of the Brazos. For, in Fulton's opinion, it was up for grabs whether Cracker's hot-tempered, doting momma or the ginger-haired spitfire he'd recently married up with was likely to take his death the hardest.

The dead boss drover's mother, Miss Melony, had been widowed young by Comanche and kept her only son out of the war betwixt the states by weeping, wailing and hiring him a substitute. Cracker's own widow, the ginger-haired Miss Dulcenia, *née* Galvez y Cabrillo of the Ox-bow Slash brand, had lost her first husband in that same war at the Battle of Franklin and sworn she'd never put herself through all that again. As a lot of water under the bridge rinsed her eyes out and time's cruel teeth got to

4

gnawing at the prettiest little spitfire they'd ever seen in those parts, she'd finally given in to the hardworking, hard-playing and hard-courting Cracker Marner, the best damned drover east or west of the Sabine and nigh as rich as any other white man in Stonewall or even King County, damn your eyes, if you wanted to bet on it.

For like the Thompson brothers and other Texas contract drovers, the late Cracker Marner had his own homespread and considerable beef herd in his own right, or, leastways, he'd registered the brand he managed for his mother, the Widow Marner, in his own name.

Combined with the original dowry herd from her own Tex-Mex family and the eight hundred head she'd received as her widow's mite when her first husband had fallen for Texas at Franklin, Tennessee, the M/G, as they'd agreed to call their consolidated holdings, since Anglo-Texicans didn't hold with those fancy Mex "scribble brands," left the two and only two surviving heirs of that one dead bully rich enough to indulge the hot tempers both were said to glory in.

According to Tiny Fulton, and later noted by worried townsmen up in Hardwater, Miss Melony had kept tabs on the Comanche Nation for many a year after her man, Cracker's Georgia-born dad, had been run over by a raiding party off the Staked Plains until, as it came to pass, that whipped and pacified Comanche Nation had been resettled on its own reserve in the Indian Territory, where a rider who could have passed for Mex or Indian paid an evening call on a former Comanche war chief and shot him down like a dog in front of his own wife and children.

Tiny Fulton couldn't say whether those yarns about a dead rebel rider's widow saving newspaper accounts of the Battle of Franklin and outlining the names of Union officers in red had been true or not. He confessed he'd

5

never seen her notorious scrapbook and that Cracker had made her get rid of it, once he'd replaced her soldier gray. But this, too, would be uneasily recalled at a second coroner's inquest, held early the following spring, after local memories of that short, sharp shoot-out in the Boxelder Saloon had faded some.

Things could go that way in Hardwater, once a deputy coroner had written up a death by gunfire at the hands of a person or persons unknown and long gone. For neither Cracker Marner's few friends or the greater number likely glad to see him dead had been able to hazard an educated guess as to just who that solitary stranger might have been or just what Cracker Marner had done to annoy him *that* much.

And so things might have remained, as an early fall gave way to a milder-than-usual winter and an unusually warm, wet greenup, with the shortgrass and pasqueflowers springing up betwixt patches of snow as it thawed, making the rolling prairie resemble the hide of a brown-and-white pinto peppered with ground parsley.

Then, around April Fool's Day, with all the snow gone and all the draws dry enough for travel again, another stranger came to Hardwater.

At the inquest to follow most witnesses would agree the second stranger who'd come in from the gathering dusk to belly up to the bar in the Boxelder had seemed taller than the first stranger and he'd worn his bigger Schofield .45-Short higher up and cross-draw.

The saloon had been less crowded and not half as smoky as it had been the night of that first shooting during the late summer trail driving. For the spring roundup only occupied riders off nearby spreads, who just got to cut, mark and brand their own stock from a consolidated local herd they'd turn loose to fatten on the thicker summer

6

grass of the North Range before a second fall roundup to cut out the market beef and drive it up Ogallala way.

Thus, since the smaller crowd assembled that evening in the Boxelder were at least familiar with one another's faces, it was hard not to notice the hawklike visage and unfriendly smile of the tall man in yet another Texican hat as he told the barkeep he'd come in for a boilermaker and a little information.

The barkeep slid a schooner of beer with a shot glass of whiskey across the zinc-topped bar as he declared he'd be proud to tell any paying customer anything they might ask, as long as he knew the answer.

The stranger swallowed the contents of the shot glass in one gulp but took his time with the chaser and never even wheezed as he calmly asked whether the barkeep had been on duty that night Cracker Marner had been gunned down by that cocksucker at that very end of the bar.

The barkeep didn't ask why the second stranger had made such a rude remark about that earlier stranger. He said he had and added he'd been right fond of the late Cracker Marner, who'd always stopped at Hardwater to rest his stock and work some of the kinks out of his own back.

The stranger quietly remarked, "Mr. Marner was a happily married man, down to Knox County, Texas, and I'll kill any son of a bitch who says he ever fooled with other women on his way to Nebraska, hear?"

The barkeep heard, and hastily assured the tall Texican they had no such unseemly affairs taking place on the premises of the Boxelder.

The surly stranger said, "I ain't here to talk about Mr. Marner's life. I've come to talk about his death. More than one rider out of Texas or the Cherokee Strip has assured

7

us that cocksucker who gunned down Mr. Marner never rode in with them. It was agreed at the inquest that the cocksucker was dressed cow. That reads to this child as if he must have come in off some nearby Kansas or Colorado spread. Ipso facto, like the lawyers say, the cocksucker must have been some rider you all had served in the past, more than once. How do you like it so far?"

The barkeep shook his head with a clear conscience to easily reply, "You're barking up the wrong tree, friend. That came up at the hearing in the Majestic Hotel up the way. I never got too grand a look at him, betwixt the overhead oil lamp and the brim of his ten-gallon hat. But I know I'd never heard his voice or served him a drink before."

The second stranger, wearing a hat the J. B. Stetson Company of Philadelphia describes as its "Boss Model," softly but firmly declared, "I don't believe you. You were standing there as close to him as you are standing close to me right now. The light would have been the same. If you can't make me out under this Stetson you need glasses or a bulls-eye lantern. Are you saying I'm a liar?"

The barkeep bristled some as he snapped back, "No, but you're sure getting mighty close to calling *me* one, friend!"

As the stranger picked up the beer schooner with his left hand to thoughtfully sip some suds, the barkeep added, "I told the coroner's jury I'd never seen that other cuss before and I'm telling you the same. Why in thunder would I want to cover up for a total asshole who gunned down a good customer like that?"

The stranger quietly decided, "Because you liked one of them more than you liked the other, you lying son of a bitch!"

Then he drew with his right hand from under his beer

and put one round in the barkeep's white shirt at point-blank range.

One round was all it took to send his victim crashing to the duckboards behind the bar, too dead to worry about his starched shirt smoldering so stinky, as the man who'd killed him swung to face the thunderghasted surviving patrons with his smoking gun muzzle trained casually in their general direction.

A lone voice in the crowd marveled, "You must be *loco en la cabeza*, Tex! You can't sashay in here like a character out of a Ned Buntline magazine and just shoot an unarmed man in cold blood!"

The man who'd done just that smiled thinly and declared, "I'll be on my way now. I advise one and all not to follow me because I am not riding solo on the lone prairie. After things calm down some another pal of mine might be riding in to ask the same sort of questions about the killing of Mr. Marner. Until then I advise one and all to reflect on what just happened to a lying bastard who tried to cover up for the one we're really after!"

The same man who'd told him he was crazy rose from his corner table to declare, "Hold on, old son. I knew poor old Gus and you had him all wrong! You can't gun a man just because, like Gus said, he couldn't say who the hell you're looking for!"

"Can *you* say who I'm looking for, friend?" the hawk-faced killer sort of purred, and when the older man, in a three-piece suit, confessed he couldn't, that Schofield bucked again and another man died in that same saloon for not knowing the answer to the same dumb question.

Then the stranger had crawfished out the bat-wing doors to vanish into the night and that might have been the end of it some more, had that second victim been the Hardwater townsman his killer had taken him for.

But he hadn't been a resident of Hardwater Township. Like both those mysterious strangers and the late Cracker Marner, he'd been passing through on other business, in his case for the federal government.

Making it a federal case.

Chapter 2

The reason the Colorado–Kansas line ran straight as a string across rolling prairie was that it had been drawn with a T square across the survey map of a once way bigger Kansas Territory to get two good-size states, populated by voters who didn't always see eye to eye.

Colorado was half high plains and half Rocky Mountains, named for its biggest river, described in Spanish for its rusty-red rapids. Kansas, like Texas, had been named for its friendliest, or least ornery, Indian nation. Western Kansas, like Eastern Colorado, was shortgrass range, recently vacated by the South Herd and Mister Lo, the Poor Indian, to make room for the cattle industry and the trail towns serving the same. Folk who plowed their land for a living got to live more closely packed, so the agricultural eastern counties of Kansas called the tune and, just recently, they'd declared Kansas a dry state. And that was how come the Boxelder Saloon and others like it could be currently found along the west end of Market Street, across the line in Colorado.

Will Chambers, the last man killed in the Boxelder by a person or persons unknown, had been riding for the

Bureau of Land Management, or Federal Land Office as it was more commonly called, as a brand inspector and recorder, listing the new brands registered along the newest as well as one of the last federal cattle trails. So once the same deputy coroner had finished *his* inquest the findings had been sent to Washington and in turn relayed to Denver, Colorado, named for a governor of the original Kansas Territory who hadn't raised too much of a fuss when a mostly mining crowd along the Front Range had voted to go their own way back in '76.

Someone at Land Management with a long memory and a desire for some damned results had suggested by name the Justice Department rider they wanted on the case. So Marshal William Vail of the Denver District Court had his clerk-typist, Henry, prepare a detailed transcript of the little information that was known, so far, and pass it on to their troubleshooting Deputy U.S. Marshal Custis Long, better known when shooting as Longarm, if one was to believe the admiring articles about him by Reporter Crawford of *The Denver Post.*

Longarm was scanning a copy of the *Kansas City Star* at his table in the Parthenon Saloon, with Henry's typed-up report, a scuttle of lager and a platter of free lunch spread before him that fine spring afternoon when his boss, the somewhat older and way shorter and fatter Billy Vail caught up with him to wearily declare, sitting down across from Longarm, "I figured you'd be here if you weren't down the hall in a file room with that pneumatic blond stenographer. Has it ever occured to you that our office is in the federal building up the way, old son?"

Longarm said, "Try one of them deviled eggs. They tanged 'em just right today. Henry told me you wanted me to read this tale of woe from the land office."

Vail snapped, "I did. But bless my soul if that don't seem to be a newspaper you've been reading instead, in

12

an infernal saloon, during your working hours, at the tax-payer's expense!"

Longarm calmly replied, "Read Henry's onionskins already. That's how come I've been hoping for more about that brand inspector in the Kansas papers. It ain't as if that coroner's report out of Hardwater contained the names and addresses of at least two killers, you know."

A Parthenon waiter came over to their side room with a pad, a pencil and an inquiring smile. Billy Vail allowed he'd have his own beer needled with bourbon and some damned warm chili con carne instead of more damned cold cuts most anybody might have prepared without washing their hands. As the waiter left, Vail pointed out, "Land Management sent us the Texas mailing addresses of at least two fine suspects: the Widows Marner, both by marriage to the late Courtney Marner and his arrowed and shot daddy. The older of the two, Miss Melony Marner née Jukes was suspected by the Bureau of Indian Affairs of holding a long, bitter grudge against the very Comanche who'd once counted coup on her husband. So how would you expect her to feel about the way more recent death of her only son?"

"Bitter," Longarm dryly replied, then added, "Don't see nothing in either this coroner's report or the *Kansas City Star* about an older woman in widow's weeds shooting anybody in that Boxelder Saloon."

Vail snorted, "Well, shit, nobody ever saw her shooting Indians on the Comanche Reserve, neither. They say the gunslick she hired looked to be another Indian, a breed or mayhaps a Mex."

Longarm nodded soberly and replied, "Wearing a tall-crowned Texican sombrero. I read evey page Henry typed. Other witnesses described the quick-draw who gunned down her little boy, Courtney a.k.a. Cracker, as a dark blur who could have been a breed under his own big Texas hat."

Vail thoughtfully chewed his unlit stogie as he studied his innocent, poker-faced senior deputy across the cluttered table, detecting not one clue as to what was going on behind those gun-muzzle gray eyes above a heroic mustache under a black-coffee Stetson, worn cavalry with its crown telescoped in a Colorado Crush. But he knew Longarm was worried about something. Longarm never looked more relaxed than when he was on edge and Vail sensed that despite the way he seemed to loll in that factory-tailored tobacco tweed frock coat with his shoe-string tie way loose for current federal dress codes, he'd cut some sign. They'd known how good he was at cutting sign when they'd asked for him by name, back East.

Their waiter came back with Vail's own order. The marshal waited until they were alone again to demand, "Spit it out. You work for me and I have a right to know."

He sipped some needled suds, nodded in satisfaction and set his own drink aside as he insisted, "You're on to something. But you ain't certain and you're hugging it close to your vest, you secretive cuss."

When Longarm didn't answer, Vail lit his cigar and wearily said, "I wish you wouldn't do that, old son. I've ofttimes shuddered, reading one of your final reports, to consider the fix you'd have left us in if you'd managed to get your fool self shot before you'd let the rest of us in on what the fuck you might have on some dangerous sons of bitches!"

Longarm thoughtfully washed down some Genoa and rat trap cheese before he confided, "I ain't cut any sensible sign. Things would cut way better if that earlier dark rider had been suspected of working for the *younger* widow, Miss Dulcenia Galvez y Cabrillo O'Brian Marner. She's from one of them old Spanish land grant clans, down

14

Texas way, and must know many a Tex-Mex rider she could call on. But her husband's *mother*, Miss Melony Marner née Jukes, would be the only one we can fairly suspect of hiring such a rider to *avenge* her own kith and kin, not to have her only spoiled rotten son blown away, right?"

Vail washed down some chili and asked to hear more about the younger of the two Widows Marner, observing, "They say she's a looker, and a redhead, despite being born a spic. You reckon that O'Brian in her family tree accounts for her hair and reputed temper?"

Longarm had been reading more carefully. He said, "Sean O'Brian was her first husband, killed at Franklin, riding with Hood's Texas Brigade. Lots of pure-white Spanish have red hair. The infamous King Phillip who sent that armada against Queen Lizzy had curly blond hair and a beard to match. I suspect Miss Dulcenia's famous temper is just plain stupidity. Dumb kids never learn to control their natural childish tempers as they grow up, and what woman with a lick of sense would have married up with Cracker Marner, for gawd's sake? From all accounts he gloried in his own infamous temper and thus we have the two of them, meeting up to court and marry on the sensible side of thirty with her unable to keep house servants and him carrying on like a school yard bully with a bullwhip in one hand and a Schofield in the other!"

Vail sipped more beer but pushed the rest of his chili aside to pick up his half-smoked stogie to chew some more as he mused, "What if, say, a hot-tempered Tex-Mex wife decided she'd made a mistake in marrying up a second time with an overgrown hot-tempered brat? What if she recruited *her* hired gun from around the headwaters of the Brazos, the same as her mother-in-law had, earlier, from the same pool of lean and hungry Tex-Mex vaqueros, or buckaroos, as Anglo-Texicans pronounce it?"

15

Longarm shrugged and pointed out, "Anything's *possible*. But once you get to scouting possible instead of logical you can end up writing books about Welsh-speaking Indians, lost Atlantis or El Dorado."

Vail protested, "Well, shit, *somebody* must have sent at least two gunslicks up to Hardwater to gun down three men in a row!"

Longarm nodded soberly and replied, "I noticed. If that smaller, darker one who gunned down Cracker Marner had been hired to lay in wait for him at Hardwater he was surely more subtle than most paid assassins. He was in that Boxelder Saloon a spell, drinking alone, when Marner came in."

Vail nodded triumphantly and said, "Just like the mysterious dark stranger expected him to. When you dry-gulch a man you get there ahead of him with your rifle-gun, see?"

Longarm shook his head and said, "There are over a dozen saloons and as many whorehouses serving liquor at the moment in Hardwater. I know the place. I likely know it better than your average Texas rider. I don't know where I'd be drinking alone like a spider waiting for its fly in any particular web over yonder."

Vail started to say something, but stalled for time by lighting another expensive but awesomely pungent cigar.

Longarm reached for a three-for-a-nickel cheroot, carried for such emergencies in a vest pocket, as he relentlessly insisted, "The witnesses all agreed Marner started up with a man who'd been drinking quiet at one end of the bar. I've considered a killer thinking ahead that clever and I just can't picture the scene as described. Cracker Marner was known to be a natural bully. But it ain't as if his killer set a trap, inviting trouble. He wasn't drinking milk or soda pop. He wasn't wearing a madras jacket with a bow tie and yaller shoes. To the extent he was recalled by anybody, he was just there, trail dusty and bearing arms but never even glancing Marner's way before the naturally mean Marner called him a bastard."

As Longarm lit his own smoke in self-defense, Vail nodded thoughtfully and decided, "That still leaves us with at least one Widow Marner as a likely suspect. Try her this way. Say the first shooting in the Boxelder Saloon went just the way the coroner's jury found. Say a spoiled brat who never grew up tried to bully the wrong school-boy. Say we leave that gunslick loosely described as a dark, quiet cuss who drank alone and didn't cotton to being decribed as a bastard. Can we agree that whoever he was he was good with a gun?"

Longarm said, "He must have been. They say the late Cracker Marner had killed his man down Texas way and put another one's eye out in Dodge with that bullwhip on another such occasion in the Alhambra."

Vail blew an octopus cloud of stinky cigar smoke as if to discourage further interruption as he continued, "*Bueno*. Let's agree that first killing was just one of those Saturday-nights-in-a-trail-town things that happen. Unless the mysterious drifter who gunned down Marner is wanted federally for something else, that killing was betwixt him and the state of Colorado. Not us."

Longarm blew a thoughtful smoke ring back at his boss and replied, "Which brings us to the late Will Chambers of the Bureau of Land Management."

"Shot by yet a second killer, decribed more thoroughly as a white man for certain, taller than average and close to your age as well."

Longarm snorted in disbelief and protested, "Aw, shit, you surely don't expect me to ride down to Texas, pre-tending to be him as we wait to see which Widow Marner offers to pay me for gunning down two poor saps I couldn't get the name of that first killer out of!"

17

Vail chuckled fondly and decided, "That would be cutting things a mite thin, but it still seems likely one or more of the Widows Marner hired that second gun to avenge the death of Cracker Marner. *That* one *told* everybody why he was shooting off his Schofield so moody. He shot the barkeep for being unwilling or unable to name that other killer and then he shot Will Chambers for insinuating he'd had no right to shoot that barkeep."

Vail shot smoke out both nostrils with a scowl before he added in a more sober tone, "Then, as I hope you noticed in Henry's transcript, the cold-blooded bastard calmly declared he or some mysterious pals would be back to ask again, and again, until somebody in Hardwater told 'em who in the hell they were looking for. So the residents of Hardwater are scared skinny or on the prod, accoring to their natures, and I don't expect you to have much trouble with anyone over yonder. So what are you waiting for, a good-bye kiss?"

Longarm grimaced and replied, "Sensible orders might be nice. According to all I've been able to glean from either these typed onionskins or the *Kansas City Star*, Will Chambers and that barkeep, Gus Henson, were shot the better part of a week ago."

Vail said, "These things take time. You ought to be able to make it to Hardwater within forty-eight hours if you get off the eastbound with your saddle at Kanorado, hire some livery stock and follow the Ogallala Trail north a ways. You won't have no trouble following that Ogallala Trail now that a few cows have been druv along it. Just follow the bare dirt and cowshit 'til you come to Hardwater, way sooner than you'd be able to drive a herd three trailbreaks north of the rails. Are there any other questions?"

Longarm said, "Yep. There's one I've wondered about ever since they opened that new Ogallala Trail. How come it runs from Texas all the way up to Ogallala, Nebraska, crossing more than one east-west railroad on it's way to them loading chutes on the U.P. Line?"

Vail said, "That's a fool question and you just answered it by naming the Union Pacific sections of the transcontinental railroad. Beef put aboard a short-line cattle car would ride all over Robin Hood's barn on its way to market, at rail-freight rates. A herd moving north to the U.P. on the hoof, grazing government grass all the way as it cuts down the distance to Omaha or Chicago, makes way more sense when you add and subtract the dollars and cents."

Vail sighed and wistfully added, "I keep trying to drum that in to you young squirts. But does anybody listen? Does anybody care that most every case boils down to love or money?"

To which Longarm could only reply, from his own experience, "Oh, I ain't so certain things always boil that pure. To begin with, you've left out pure insanity."

Chapter 3

Despite its name, the railroad town of Kanorado lay mostly well inside the dry state of Kansas. So Longarm felt no call to linger in Kanorado longer than he had to. He'd found in earlier travels along the Ogallala Trail that Kansas could be most picky about such matters near its borders with wet states. Nobody in Dodge City, well within the undivided jurisdiction of the Kansas state courts, paid mind to the matter and you could still order anything from near beer to 100 proof at the wide-open Alhambra or more intimate Long Branch.

Since it was not a federal matter whether Kansas state lawmen might or might not be in cahoots or outright owners of Kansas saloons, Longarm carried his McClellan saddle and possibles directly from the railroad platform to the nearest livery stable, determined to get out of town before dark, lest he spend the night there dry. He knew that if he rode some he could make the next town, twelve miles north, before ten that evening. He knew that once he had, he'd find the saloons on the west side of town just starting to get interesting.

He wasn't looking for a chatty crowd in a neighborhood

saloon because he felt lost and friendless on the Ogallala Trail. He knew both those killers farther north in Hardwater had worn Texican hats, and had likely passed through this same country the same way. So, as that second killer had surmised, more than one old boy in more than one location could have seen that first killer, months earlier, if only one could inspire them to remember the son of a bitch.

Longarm knew he had an edge or more on that second hardcase somebody had sent after the first one. Longarm was trying to cut the sign of *two* who'd gone before him and, in the case of that second certain white man wearing that army surplus Schofield .45-Short, he had a better description of a more recent passage.

Billy Vail had said, and Longarm had agreed, the man who'd killed Will Chambers, a federal employee, was more important to any federal court than a dark blur who'd gunned down a total asshole nobody but his wife and mother seemed to give a shit about.

At the livery, Longarm chose a chestnut barb and a paint cayuse, both of the shemale persuasion, a tad long in the tooth, as one had to expect from livery stock, but well shod and sounding full of air instead of mucus when he thumped their barrels with the heel of his palm.

As he was settling up with the livery manager on the six bits a day and somewhat stiff deposits, Longarm quietly suggested that he only meant to ride up to Hardwater and back with the ladies and had no intention of eloping with either.

The older gent he was dickering with wearily replied, "I just work here. I know who you are and why you're here, Mr. Longarm. So if it was up to me alone I'd be proud to trust you for the stock. But we've been losing ponies here in Kanorado. So the folk I work for gave me

21

orders to make it worth a customer's while to bring the damned old hired ponies *back*."

Longarm said, "I heard the price of cows and cowponies were on the rise. But a fifty-dollar deposit on two retired cowponies is downright silly. Where could you sell either of these sweet old ladies for any twenty-five whole dollars?"

The livery manager smiled smugly and explained, "Nowheres we could think of. That's why we hold more than they're worth until we get 'em back. Don't glare at me like that, Mr. Longarm. Like I said, I just work here and, to date, we've lost three or four good mounts to customers who left more modest deposits and never came back."

Longarm almost let that pass. Then he draped his heavily laden army saddle over a handy corral rail and got out his notebook and a pencil stub to back the livery manager to the beginning of his tale of woe, a good eight months earlier, when a customer described as a "usual Texas rider, mayhaps a tad darker and, let's see, a Colt, I reckon, worn low and sidedraw," had ridden off on a blue roan branded Double Diamond X and never returned it, forfeiting his fifteen-dollar deposit.

Then, more recently, a week or so ago, two gents with Texas hats had ridden off aboard a buckskin gelding and a cordovan mare, leaving twenty in trust for each hired mount, never to be seen again.

Once he'd gone over it again and committed those brands to paper as well, Longarm put his book away, musing, "Not one of the three rode all the way up from Texas. Not along the Ogallala Trail, leastways. First the lone dark one and then the two trying to track him down must have got off an eastbound or westbound here in Kanorado. Either works as well, so far. Had any of them arrived on horseback they'd have had no call to hire one from you."

The livery manager suggested, "What if one or more

rode his pony into the ground and felt the need for a fresh mount?"

Longarm shook his head and demurred, "Has anybody seen such a pony, dead or alive, within walking distance of here?"

The livery manager allowed he followed Longarm's drift. So they shook on the deal and Longarm was on his way, riding the barb he'd saddled first and leading the paint for later.

He was riding the paint and leading the barb when they got into Rusty Springs well after sundown. As a man who'd ridden some, Longarm saw to both ponies being watered and fed (Never the other way around!) and rubbed down before he tipped the grinning stable hands extra to stall them for the night indoors and away from the tricky night winds one got on the high plains at greenup time.

Then he headed for the west side of town to find a lively place to ask a heap of casual questions. As he was about to enter one brightly lit card house he heard the tinkle of an upright piano from across the way and paused to turn and stare that way, thoughtful, as he decided he had to be hearing right.

Nobody on God's green earth played a piano that strange, or screwed any better, than the one and original Miss Red Robin of Chicago and just about everywhere west of the same, since she'd treated a boss just awful for putting a hand up her skirt without her permission.

Longarm hesitated because he knew Billy Vail had never sent him to the Ogallala Trail to trifle with such a bodacious bawd. Then he went on over after reflecting on how much gossip one might hear playing for the locals in a neighborhood saloon.

He hadn't been getting any lately, either.

As he drifted into the less-brightly lit and not-too-crowded Rabbit's Foot Concert Hall with bottled beer on ice, the Junoesque gal of around thirty seated at the upright with her bare back to the entrance naturally failed to see him. So, with her henna-rinsed hair pinned high above the exposed nape of her neck, her red velveteen ballroom gown open down to the small of her back, the aptly descibed Miss Red Robin went on singing as she hammered at the out-of-tune or ill-treated piano . . .

> "You may talk about your Beauregard;
> And sing of General Lee.
> But the gallant Hood of Texas;
> Played hell in Tennessee!"

That had been what Longarm had suspected from across the way that she might have been shooting for, even though the tune sounded more like "Yellow Rose of Texas" than "Marching Through Georgia" whenever others tried for it. He knew Red Robin had hatched or invented herself around Chicago and both Colorado and Kansas had been Union states while Hood's Texas Brigade had been raising all that hell in Tennessee. So he surmised Red Robin had to be playing by request and had no trouble spotting more than one likely Texican amid the crowd assembled that night in the Rabbit's Foot.

By that late in the game most cowhands dressed a heap the same for sensible reasons. The *Police Gazette* and *Ned Buntline's Wild West* notwithstanding, riders drawing steady pay for honest effort dressed for their chores, rather than to frighten Indians. Cotton clung more comfortably to the unwashed hide of a hard-riding hand better than most other textiles. Men who rode standing in their stirrups aboard a zigzagging roping or cutting pony favored high heels less to look tall than to keep from getting dragged after slipping a booted ankle all the way through a stirrup as they fell off. Tight pants of duck or denim chafed less against saddle leather. Loose shirts of thinner cotton left a workingman's arms and chest room to twist and turn as need be. Most cowhands as well as the U.S. Cav west of, say, longitude 100° wore loose neckerchiefs to wipe sweaty brows or tie over their muzzles to breathe through when the going got dry and dusty. But after that there came regional differences, because the chores were not everywhere the same.

North Range hands rode through cooler but way wilder winds and thus wore their hats crushed tighter to their skulls lest they kite away at full gallop. Down Texas way the air hung still or came at you all at once as dust devils or worse. So Tex-Mex riders favored high-crowned sombreros with broader and shadier brims to keep their poor brains from frying. Working closer to the original blue print of the pure Mexican vaquero, the Tex-Mex rider cinched his saddle center-fire and roped in the dally style the vaquero had learned from his North African and Aztec predecessors. The Moors had introduced the longhorn cow along with a heap of herding practices to Old Spain. Then Spanish settlers herding cows in New Spain had noticed how slick some recently converted mission Aztec could rope anything on four legs, from a dog to a deer, with braided rawhide throw ropes and combined the two skills as Mexican dally roping, still favored by everyone south of the Arkansas Divide.

Dally roping was easier on the stock but harder to master. So most North Range riders, coming west later from states with no Mex notions about working stock, had adopted the pure advantages of the throw rope, but favored the rougher and easier to learn tie-down style, cinching their flatter roping saddles fore and aft to take the shock as the roped critter hit the end of a stiffer but stronger grass rope with a jerk that tended to drop it to the sod, if it failed to jerk the pony down as well.

As a natural result of such different roping styles, although both called for much the same riding duds, the Texican looked different at both ends, with his high-crowned hat offset by his bodacious spurs.

Texicans didn't wear spurs that jingled and jangled when they walked so's the gals could hear them coming. A dally roper needed both hands holding his rope, steering with his spurs as he let the reins ride loose across his mount's withers. So his spurs had to gain his mount's undivided attention.

No sensible rider aimed to *hurt* any horse with a spur. So the big jangling rowels of the Tex-Mex spur, sun-bursted with too many points for any one to dig in, seemed to goose-bump a loping pony into turning just as tight with a loose bit in its lathered jaws.

The tie-down roper on the North Range never let go of the reins he held in one hand with mayhaps a few loose coils of his throw rope as he swung the noose with the other. So *his* spurs served only to make his mount run faster when he dug both in at once on either side. Hence his silent spurs were designed along more military lines with smaller but somewhat crueler rowels that didn't jingle lest they spook a pony into running when no running might be called for.

It wasn't possible to check spurs below table level as Longarm stood by the bar to one side of Red Robin, waiting for her to glance his way in her own good time. But he made out seven high-crowned sombreros in the crowd of mayhaps two dozen all told. Longarm suspected the Texas hands had come in together. Red Robin wouldn't have been singing the praises of Gallant Hood of Texas had only one or two Texicans requested her to in a mostly North Range saloon. Longarm ordered a schooner of suds and nursed it, a faint curl to his lips, as he noted how one of the tall-hatted riders in a red-and-black checkered shirt was beating time under the table with what sounded like key chains attached to his thudding high heels. Longarm had nothing against the Gallant Hood of Texas, who'd recently died of the yellow jack in New Orleans and been gallant enough in his day to go on fighting after he'd had an arm crippled at Gettysburg and lost a whole leg at Chickamauga. But Hood had been the real thing and that squirt in the checked shirt was too young to have served on either side, despite his stomps and the rebel yell he let fly as Red Robin finished.

Longarm forgot the noisy kid when, as he'd hoped, Red Robin glanced his way, past the brandy snifter atop her piano for tips, and sprang up to run at him like a football tackle out to flatten somebody. So it was just as well Longarm had the bar at his back to brace him as he caught her with his one free arm and they kissed natural as old pals might in such an awkward position.

Red Robin kissed way better than she played the piano. She did most anything better than she played the piano. Longarm set his beer on the bar to grab her wrist as she seemed to be trying to unbutton his fly in front of everybody.

As they came up for air, the sultry Red Robin demanded, "Custis Long, what in blue blazes are you doing here in Rusty Springs? Who told you I'd been engaged here at the Rabbit's Foot, you horny thing?"

Idly wondering why she was laying it on so heavy, Longarm refrained from rudely replying he'd had no idea she was anywheres east of the Front Range. He gallantly replied they'd told him down in Kanorado and so, seeing he was headed north on a field mission, he'd thought he might as well stop by to drop in on her.

Before she could answer, a pouty male voice to Longarm's right declared, "You are out of line, Mr. Whiskey

Drummer in the pretty suit and porkpie hat. For I seen her first and there's two whole dollars of mine in her fucking brandy glass to prove it."

Red Robin pulled away from Longarm to get between them, laughing too hard to mean it as she assured them both there was more than enough there for all her friends.

The kid laughed back, uncertain, to ask if she really meant that.

But Longarm shoved Red Robin out of their line of fire, informing the nineteen- or-twenty-year-old boy in no uncertain terms, "If she meant it you'd still be out of luck. You ain't my type. I'll give you your two dollars back. I'll even buy you and all your pals a round. But if you ever use such language in front of a lady in my presence again you'll find yourself in a whole lot of trouble."

The slightly tipsy and very mixed-up kid stepped back a pace to brace himself on widespread boot heels, his gun hand hovering above the cherry grips of his Paterson Conversion as he snarled, "I'll be the judge of who might be a lady and who might be in trouble, here!"

Longarm followed his drift as half a dozen Texas hats rose as one to slowly but surely head his way, while others who'd been listening sort of tensely to that old Texas marching song proceeded to vacate the premises suddenly.

Chapter 4

Two of the Texicans backing the kid's play looked Anglo. The other four seemed Cado, Mex or both. The assimilated Cado Nation of Texas tended to speak Spanish more often than English, albeit the tall, good-looking one in the black whipcord *charro* outfit and *buscadero* gun belt spoke fair English as he announced, "I was paying attention, so I feel for you, Señor. There is no argument that Junior Brown, here, has some growing up to do. But what else can we do? We ride for his most worried father and we have orders for to keep him alive in spite of himself."

Longarm nodded in as friendly a manner as the situation called for and replied, "We were all as young, one time, and since no harm's been done, why don't we all have a drink to General Hood and peace at last?"

The tall, saturnine Mex shook his head sadly to say, "Before I tell you how we're going to end this *tonterias*, allow me for to introduce myself. I am called Miguelito del Pecos and whether you have heard of me or not I wish for you to leave, now—*poco tiempo*—with no argument, eh?"

Longarm told Red Robin to leave the room. The kid

who'd thought he could buy more than a marching song for two dollars grinned like a shit-eating dog and marveled, "Oh, hot damn, we're going to have us a hot time in the old town, tonight."

And they might have, had not another rider of the Mex persuasion called urgently, *"No, esperate! Penso el no es un chulo. Penso es un pistolero peligroso!"*

Longarm was too smart to let on he could follow the drift of Border Mex and, even though she'd ignored his order to light out, Red Robin was too smart to let on she knew that.

So neither changed expression as the one called Miguelito stared thoughtfully at Longarm to softly muse aloud, *"Pues . . . no sé, Emilio."*

The one called Emilio insisted, *"Sin falta! Penso El Brazo Largo!"*

To which Miguelito could only reply, *"Ay, mierda, vámonos pa'l carajo!* You too, Junior Brown. They only pay me to keep you alive, not to die for you. So is time for to move it on down the pike, as your own kith and kin put it."

The kid in the checked shirt was still arguing with them as Miguelito and the short and stout one who'd recognized Longarm frog-marched their spoiled brat outside to leave the Rabbit's Foot deserted, save for themselves, two bewildered barkeeps and a colored swamper peering anxiously out from a back room as the tobacco smoke commenced to slowly clear.

When the barkeep who served as night manager demanded to know what in thunder had happened to all their customers Red Robin told him he'd just had a narrow brush with being shut down for a spell, explaining, "Those Texas rowdies were fixing to shoot it out with this federal lawman standing here. Do I need to tell you what might have happened to your liquor license even if you tried to open up again after such a serious inquest?"

The night manager allowed that in that case they could all use a nightcap. It was Red Robin, herself, who wanted to know how Longarm had been able to back seven armed and dangerous drunks down without even drawing on them. He nodded his thanks as the night manager slid some personal malt liquor across the mahogany to them and told Red Robin he wasn't sure, since he hadn't been able to follow all that Spanish, and she let it go.

That was another thing Longarm liked about Red Robin. For a woman, she played poker swell. So they'd always gotten along well since first she'd tried to kill him, down Texas way, mistaking him for a lawman on her trail when all he'd wanted to do was screw her.

Once they'd gotten all that straightened out they'd discovered to their mutual delight that neither was inclined to press a pillow conversation beyond natural curiosity to personal prying. Thus Longarm had never determined Red Robin's real name or natural hair coloring and neither had ever asked the other where they'd learned to fornicate so fine. As they stood there sharing good stuff with the night manager Longarm knew Red Robin knew he spoke tolerable Border Mex. Just as he knew she'd never ask that question again until she knew he was ready to answer.

That moment came sooner than it might have, had Junior Brown and his pals been content to just listen to Red Robin's grotesque piano playing. For the Rabbit's Foot would have stayed open past midnight if anybody else had been there, paying for the overhead. But as they waited in vain for business to pick up some more the only others who came through the bat-wing doors were the town marshal and two deputies armed with shotguns.

The portly town marshal, a barbed wire drummer when he wasn't called on to uphold the law and order in those parts, came warily over to say, "Tod Woods tells us you were fixing to have a shoot-out over this way. Have we missed the fun?"

The night manager suggested they ask Longarm, since he'd missed a lot of the conversation.

Longarm nodded modestly and said, "It was no big deal, Marshal. I'm the law, too. Deputy U.S. Marshal Custis Long of the Denver District Court. This young cowboy who'd had too much to drink took exception to this fool necktie they've made me wear since President Hayes got elected on that reform ticket. Fortunately his pals talked him out of it and carried him away to sober up."

The town marshal said, "The way I hear it, the whole bunch just rode out of town as if fleeing for their lives. Tod Woods says the fight was over Miss Red Robin, here."

Longarm shrugged and suggested, "That was my fault. I asked the kid not to use bad language in here because they had a lady playing their piano. Miss Red Robin had nothing to do with the slight misunderstanding."

The town law stared thoughtfully at Red Robin and decided, "If you say so. I've seen your name on the front pages of the *Rocky Mountain News* and so far be it from me to call the famous Longarm a liar. You surely inspired some sudden night riding when those Texicans realized just who they'd started up with. What brings you here to Rusty Springs, Deputy Long?"

Longarm answered truthfully and easily, "Just passing through. You likely heard about that recent shooting up to Hardwater. One of the men shot worked for Uncle Sam and they want me to see what can be done about that."

The law of Rusty Springs said, "I feel for you but I just can't reach you, pard. They possed up to track that total stranger in town during an otherwise quiet spell. When you get there I know what they're fixing to tell you. They're fixing to tell you they cut no sign on the open range all around and found nobody willing to admit to sheltering at least two men and their ponies when they canvased a day's ride in every direction. I know all this because they canvased this far south and beyond. The killer and his sidekick are long gone."

"That's likely why they left no sign, crossing recently thawed and still soft prairie loam under tender greenup grass. The way I read it, the most recent killer was there asking questions about that earlier killer he was anxious to have a word with. I never read anything about anybody answering his questions and he seemed to feel that one he was after was still hiding out, somewhere near Hardwater," Longarm said.

He downed his shot glass, gasped for air and added, "But like the old song says, further along we'll know more about it and so for now we'll just have to wait and see."

The town law agreed that seemed to be about the size of it. So he and his deputies had to be included in another round of the poor night manager's private stock. But he managed a gallant smile as he declared he was closing for the night before they went bankrupt.

Red Robin had hired quarters over a carriage house up a back alley. It was her suggestion they leave by the back door whilst the swamper shut and barred the front entrance. Since the town law had told them those seven Texas riders had left town, Longarm figured she didn't want anybody gossiping about a henna-rinsed gal in a low-cut red gown leading strange men astray up back alleys.

Once she had him at her mercy in the perfumed darkness of her cozy hired quarters Red Robin waited until she had them both stripped bare as babes and working on their second coming, dog style, before she got around to asking about that tense scene in the tap room again.

As Longarm stood by the bed with his bare feet on the rug and a well-padded hipbone in either hand to haul her on and off his raging erection like a tight, wet, velvet glove, he modestly confided, "There's no great mystery, honey. They had me down as another drunk their boss man's son had started up with. Then that short and stocky one told them who I was. Some other Mex must have pointed me out to him, closer to the border. *El Brazo Largo* translates as The Long Arm in Spanish. For some reason that seems to excite some Mexicans down along the border."

Red Robin arched her spine to thrust her soft but still shapely rump higher as she replied, "Mmmm, nice! I read something in *The Denver Post* about you causing an international incident down Mexico way. How come you and some Mex pals had to wipe out that one army column?"

He thrust deeply, enjoying the new angle as much as she did as he told her, "There was only that one army column after us. I wasn't down yonder to tangle with the current Mex dictatorship. I was after one of our own public enemies. But as in the case of you mistaking me for some Chicago lawman after you, that time, El Presidente Diaz and his own bunch keep assuming I'm out to overthrow his stable government, as Wall Street describes it. Why don't we roll you over on your pretty little back and swap some spit as we finish this right?"

Red Robin, as ever, was willing to try anything that didn't hurt and so a grand time was had by all as they went at it belly to belly and mouth to mouth, enjoying the aftertase of malt liquor as they attempted to tie their tongues into a lover's knot. You didn't need a pillow under Red Robin's ass in that position because in point of fact she was getting a tad broad across the hips from spreading her bottom across so many piano stools across the West. A piano-playing gal who could have used piano lessons and never wanted to fuck her boss got to move across the West a lot.

As they indulged her in another bad habit—smoking in bed after one hell of a screwing—Longarm silently reflected on how discreet Miss Red Robin was at other times, despite the effect they seemed to have on one another. They'd established early on that neither was after more than a few tender moments with somebody they could level with before they'd passed on again like ships in the night. Unlike some of his other pals of the shemale persuasion, Red Robin never asked who he might have had his old organ grinder inside of since last he'd shoved it in *her*, and she'd been honest and open that one time she'd had to tell him plain out that she'd made other plans with another man when he'd been expecting a warmer welcome in another lonely little trail town. So the next time they'd met up again Longarm had never asked how things had gone with that other man and her welcome in *that* lonely little trail town had been warm indeed.

But there were natural limits to any woman's discretion and so as they cuddled against the bed board, passing one of his three-for-a-nickel cheroots back and forth, Red Robin asked when he figured on heading up to that other lonely little trail town called Hardwater.

Longarm answered honestly, since that was the best policy with any woman with common sense, "Meant to be on my way come sunup. Didn't know this much temptation would be in my way. Am I correct in assuming you mean to sleep past noon, report back to work in the afternoon and thump that piano past midnight?"

Red Robin sighed and said, "I doubt I'll *sleep* past noon. I can see you ain't been getting any lately, neither. Am *I* correct in assuming you ain't about to wait around all day and half the night for just a little more of all I have to offer?"

Longarm sighed and passed her the smoke so he could nibble her ear as he reluctantly confided, "I'm fixing to catch hell for wiring my boss so late from Hardwater, tomorrow evening. It's going to take me that long to get there if I ride out of here after noon. But I doubt a few stolen hours are likely to make much difference. You haven't heard any local gossip I could use about that recent shooting up in Hardwater, have you? I followed the dulcet sounds of your fine piano playing when it occured to me you talk to your customers a lot."

Red Robin snuggled closer as she purred, "I'll bet that was what you were after, you nosey thing. I've naturally heard lots of talk about a shooting just up the trail. But I haven't heard any guesses that made more sense than you and the town law were making, back by the bar. You just now scared seven gun toters back to Texas, you growly thing. Do you really expect just a pair at most to linger around Hardwater, with you on the way?"

Longarm snubbed out the smoke and commenced to roll one of her nipples betwixt thumb and forefinger as he replied, "Let's hope they ain't expecting me, or ain't scared of me, then."

Meanwhile, an easy day's ride up the Ogallala Trail, the tall, hawk-faced rider, with a Schofield .45-Short drawn and cocked in one big fist, was covering two terrified stable hands with the same as they cowered in the tack room under a flickering ceiling lamp that needed more coal oil.

One of the young hands was a white boy, the other was an Osage breed. The much taller and somewhat older white man covering them with his unwavering gun muzzle was saying, "I ain't fixing to ask it again. Was there or was there not a blue roan branded Double Diamond X on or about these premises last summer?"

The white boy stammered, "I already told you, mister. I wasn't working here last summer. So how the hell would I know?"

The tall stranger shot him at point-blank range, sending him over a racked saddle in a backward somersault to land dishrag limp on the far side as the cold-eyed killer swung his smoking muzzle to cover the breed kid and purr, "I'm sure you can do better than that, Chief."

Young Bobby Arrowmaker knew he was about to die and this made his eyes sting but he managed not to cry and before he answered, he took a deep breath, let it half out, so his voice wouldn't crack as he stared stone faced at the unwavering eye of .45 caliber death to reply in an almost dreamy tone, "Hear me. It is true we have become Christians. I know you see me standing here in the clothing of the *Wasichu* and it is true I have never counted coup in the Osage manner. But I am still, by *Wakan Tanka*, at least half Osage and so you can just take a running fuck at a rolling donut before I'll tell you shit!"

Chapter 5

"How did you do that?" gasped the killer as he fired blind in total darkness, then fired twice more, lower, for luck.

In the ear-ringing silence that followed, the man left standing there in brimstone-scented blackness inquired in a falsely caring tone if his little pal was hurt bad.

Bobby Arrowmaker didn't answer. He hadn't really wanted to die. So when that flickering overhead lamp had winked out he'd crabbed sideways before rolling behind a nail keg that seemed too small by half and held his breath with all his might.

Outside under prairie stars, doors and windows commenced to pop open and other lamps winked on all over Hardwater. So the killer snarled, "If you're still there, we'll be having this same conversation again and you'd best study hard on that blue roan and the cocksucker riding it, you sassy-lipped redskin!"

Then he was out the door and his spurs jingled off in the night to where Bobby Arrowmaker felt it safe to strike a match and discover that as he'd feard, Luke Warner lay dead as a turd in a milk bucket, and old Luke had been all right, for a fucking *Wasichu*.

So he'd held nothing back about his sidekick's cold-blooded murder or the tall, hawk-faced Texas rider who'd gunned him. Nobody at the coroner's inquest asked what the breed kid might know about that earlier customer who might have left a blue roan in their care the summer before. So Bobby Arrowmaker didn't have to lie to anybody about that customer who'd come back in a hurry for his mount after a shoot-out in the Boxelder Saloon. He'd have had to lie, had they asked him, for who but a drunken wife-seller would turn in a man of his own kind just for killing a *Wasichu?* Bobby Arrowmaker had no idea why that older man dressed like a Texas trailherd had shot that Texas trailboss that late summer night just down the way; there were things one did not ask another Osage when he returned in a hurry, early, to mount up and ride by moonlight. From the little he'd heard later about the shooting that one called Marner had had it coming. He'd probably called that other Osage "Chief."

Bobby Arrowsmith hated it when *Wasichu* did that, grinning at him like they were tossing a bone to a yard dog.

So they were expecting Longarm at the Municipal Corral and Livery Services when he rode into Hardwater after sundown, somewhat recovered after a good hard ride in the saddle instead of in Red Robin. They knew he'd naturally be tending first to the needs of his ponies after that much time on the trail.

An older, white man with an iron mustache explained as he tended to Longarm's riding stock how he'd lost one of his night hands to a round of .45-Short and told the other to stay home on paid leave until they caught Luke Warner's killer.

He explained, "Bobby Arrowmaker was the one and only witness to the cold-blooded killing and the heartless son of a bitch told Bobby he'd be back! Ain't that a bitch?"

Longarm replied, "It sure is. They sent me here to look into the death of a brand inspector called Will Chambers."

The liveryman said, "Same killer, as best the deputy coroner and his panel were able to make out this afternoon. He said he or some of his pals would be back when he gunned down that government man last week and Bobby Arrowmaker's description of him fits the ones given by survivors in the Boxelder Saloon. He must be hovering somewhere out on the open range, like a low-flying buzzard. Because nobody's been able to cut his sign and he sure keeps coming back!"

"If it's the same rider," Longarm pointed out, asking whether Bobby Arrowmaker had been present at both shootings.

The liveryman shook his head and said his night hand had only seen that hawk-faced rascal the other night, but added, "How many hawk-faced rascals wearing high-crowned Texas hats and packing Schofield horse pistols do you reckon we might have in these parts?"

Longarm dryly replied, "No more than two. It's been my sad experience that witnesses often see what witnesses expect to see and this Bobby Arrowmaker had heard others describe a hawk-faced killer packing an army pistol before he saw his sidekick murdered in cold blood. So what else can you tell me about this Bobby Arrowmaker? He'd be a full-blood, right?"

The man young Arrowmaker worked for shook his head and answered, "Wrong. Him and his big sister, Sally, are Osage breeds. She works as a chambermaid at the Majestic Hotel up the way. He works here when he ain't laid low by death threats. They're both good kids, for breeds. As honest as some white kids I could mention. I doubt Bobby would describe things different than he saw 'em. He was sure about that army gun. He's always admired the U.S. Cav his daddy rode with."

Longarm frowned and said, "I'm missing something here. Cherokee take the names of their maternal clans. Osage living traditional just use personal names and never mention the names of dead elders if they can possibly avoid it. So whilst some assimilated Osage have taken to using their dad's personal name as a family name . . ."

"I follow your drift," the liveryman cut in, explaining, "it's a natural confusion. Them two breed kids were sprinkled Christian with Arrowmaker as their last name because their dad was Sergeant Arrowmaker of the Osage Scouts. He went under at the Battle of Pea Ridge, fighting for the Union against Rebel Cherokee, see?"

Longarm said, "Not hardly. Are you saying they had a white *momma*, married to a Quill Indian?"

The liveryman nodded and replied, "Miss Sally Kellerman. Named her daughter after her own self and her son, Bobby, after a kid brother killed by the same Comanche who kidnapped her when she was little. The rangers rescued her before she'd had any half-Comanche kids. But not before she'd lost her cherry, Comanche-style, more than once. So, whilst she was a pretty little thing . . ."

"No white man would marry up with her." Longarm nodded, familiar with a tale that only varied in detail with each telling.

The liveryman sighed and said, "We're talking a spell back before the war, when folk out our way were even pickier about such notions. So whilst I never knew either, personally, it's come down to us through the years that Sergeant Arrowmaker was a Christian convert who could read and write. They say he courted an outcast white gal quite a spell with gentle good humor until he got her to marry up with him. Sort of. They got an easygoing Papist

41

priest to marry them up in the eyes of his furrin' church, whether the State of Kansas approved such marriages or not. I understand Miss Sally raised her resulting kids in the Papist faith. Sort of. There ain't no Papist church around here and she herself had been sprinkled Methodist before the Comanche ruined her."

Longarm said, "I savvy the Indian surname, now. I'll take your word the Arrowmakers are a respected local family."

The local resident shook his head and said, "No, they ain't. Like I said, Sergeant Arrowmaker fell for the Union years ago and the elder Miss Sally's been gone for six or eight summers. Died of some shemale complaint the sawbones couldn't do nothing for. So such family as there may be consists of no more than the results of a sad love story, the younger Miss Sally and the hardworking Bobby, who's never lied to me yet."

Longarm decided, "I'll keep your commendation in mind when I talk to him about that recent killing. I'm sure my boss will want me to make a federal case out of it, seeing the killer sounds like the same one we're after for the shooting of that federal brand inspector."

They shook on that and parted friendly. Longarm had learned not to ask one witness all the questions and he had a heap of courtesy calls he'd have to make in a mighty small town.

It was getting late to come calling on witnesses he hadn't been introduced to, in any case. Pounding on the door of folk worried about a killer who'd promised to come back, this late of an evening, could be injurious to one's health.

So Longarm toted his saddlebags and Winchester '73 on up to the Majestic Hotel, having entrusted his McClellan saddle and army bridle to the livery along with his hired ponies.

The optimistically named Majestic Hotel was built more along the lines of a gigantic soap box, with its balloon frame enclosed in board and baton sheathing that could have used another coat of whitewash where it wasn't perforated by vertical sash windows with park-bench green shutters. Such shutters were not just for show to either side of any windows exposed to the uncertain winds of the open range along the Ogallala Trail.

But the spring breezes were well behaved that evening as Longarm stowed his possibles and tempting saddle gun in his hired corner room and locked up, for the moment, as he discreetly wedged a match stem under the bottom hinge before moscying back downstairs for a late supper and the feeling of a town he hadn't been through for a spell.

First things coming first, and just hating to have his suppers horned in on by pesky local lawmen, Longarm headed on over to the town marshal's office where, as he'd hoped, he found nobody more important than a kid deputy keeping one eye on their one prisoner in the drunk tank and the other on the front door as he presided over the night blotter on the desk in front of him.

When Longarm introduced himself the kid said, "We've been expecting you. Marshal Breen's left for the night, but if there's anything I can do for you, just name it, Deputy Long."

Longarm made the kid feel more important than he was by asking for some names and addresses to write down in his own notebook. When the kid allowed they'd saved him a carbon of the coroner's findings that afternoon Longarm gravely accepted the same and asked the kid for a name of his own to put down for an assistance.

The lawman of, say, twenty-odd years grinned as if he'd just hooked a bluegill and said he was Deputy Colson. Timothy Colson, except that everybody had always called him Tim.

Longarm asked which he preferred. The kid seemed surprised by having any say-so, then decided if Tim was good enough for his pals it was good enough for him.

They shook on that and Longarm was free to amble on for that mighty late supper, his empty gut agrowl as he explored a ways and decided on a narrow-gauge chili parlor with barely room for the counter and row of stools running back from the open front.

Longarm chose a stool near the back wall and bet the fat short-order cook of Hispanic persuasion that they couldn't rustle him up some *huevos rancheros* over most any kind of steak.

When the fat Mex asked whether he'd care for T-bone or a New York cut Longarm said he didn't care as long as it came rare. He confided that he preferred his steaks no more than gravely injured and the fat Mex allowed he might be able to manage that.

As he got to work on the order Longarm scanned the not-too-tedious findings of the inquest they'd been holding in his hotel lobby whilst he'd been trying to get there from Rusty Springs that afternoon. Having no way of knowing any better, Longarm found it easy enough to buy the testimony of young Bobby Arrowmaker, who'd simply stated that a total stranger fitting the description of the man who'd gunned Gus Henson and Will Chambers down, earlier, in the Boxelder, had busted in on them with his gun already drawn whilst they'd been playing checkers in the tack room at the Municipal Corral and Livery Services.

When a member of the coroner's jury had asked the breed kid how long he'd worked there, seeing the stranger had shot poor Luke Warner for saying he was new on the job, Bobby Arrowmaker had allowed he'd worked there

44

going on three years and his boss, a Chester Bedford who was likely that older gent with the iron mustache, had backed the boy up. When asked how he'd answered that same question from the nosey cuss with the big .45, Bobby Arrowmaker had answered simply that all hell had busted loose before he'd been asked how long he'd worked there. The young breed had opined, sounding a tad defensive, that the stranger had doubtless taken the late Luke Warner for the senior and boss stable hand because he'd been a paleface.

Longarm made a mental note that, like more than one breed he'd brushed with in the past, this Bobby Arrowmaker seemed to carry that same tedious chip on his shoulder.

A heap of breeds did. It wasn't entirely their own fault. For even the easygoing Mark Twain had remarked in his book about Tom Sawyer that there was just no trusting a half-breed. So Twain's villainous Indian Joe had combined all the vices and none of the virtues of both races as he scared poor Tom and his blond Becky Thatcher for no sensible reasons an honest whiteman or a noble redman would have come up with.

Musing about such matters almost made Longarm miss the part about that stranger waving a gun at them over a blue roan branded Double Diamond X. Longarm didn't have to consult his notebook to recall that liveryman in Kanorado had so described a mount hired from them the summer before and never returned. Bobby Arrowmaker had testified he couldn't recall half the ponies left overnight with them over the course of half that time. But Longarm could see that if the mysterious deadly stranger was asking about a livery pony hired out the summer before, about the time of that first shooting in the Boxelder, he was likely the same cuss pestering Gus Henson and Will Chambers about yet another mysterious stranger who well may have ridden in aboard a blue roan and then ridden out on the same, since no such mount had ever been noticed, dead or alive, along this stretch of the Ogallala Trail.

The short-order-cook-cum-counter-man slid Mexican eggs over a New York steak, rare, across the oilcloth at him. So Longarm put all his paperwork away as he allowed he'd have black coffee with his supper.

He'd just dug in when he noticed another customer moving in from the dark street out front. It was a public beanery and thus no beeswax of a federal lawman whether anyone else wanted *huevos rancheros* or not.

Then he noticed the newcomer, coming all the way back to where he was seated, was that Miguelito del Pecos, still wearing that same big hat, *charro* outfit and *buscadero* gun belt, loaded for bear with a brace of Colt thumbuster .45-40s.

So Longarm nodded pleasantly and said, "Howdy. Great minds seem to run in the same channels and these *huevos rancheros* ain't bad."

To which Miguelito del Pecos replied with a sort of fatalistic smile, "*No me jodas, Gringo.* I know who you are and I know what they say about you. But since you have followed us all this way for to dance with me, by the beard of Christ, you shall dance with me here and now! So *chinge tu madre* or go for your gun, you *hijo de puta*! For to me it makes no difference!"

Chapter 6

Longarm's voice was friendly but firm as he said, "Just you sit by my side if you love me, with both hands on the counter if you don't want to sing soprano in the time it takes a gut-shot *pendejo* to die!"

So Miguelito del Pecos did as he was told, managing not to sob as he quietly asked, "How did you do that, *El Brazo Largo*?"

Longarm moved the muzzle of his .44-40 from the *segundo*'s pubic bone to a floating rib as he replied, not unkindly, "Later. First we have to clear some bullshit up. To begin with I never followed you boys up this way from Rusty Springs. I'm here on more serious beeswax and I'll ask you to consider how easy it would have been for me to kill you, just now, with me packing a badge in my own neck of the woods whilst you spouted open invites to a shoot-out. Are you with me so far?"

When the Tex-Mex just sat there with his own guns out of reach Longarm said, *"Bueno,"* and called the counter man back to order a plate of the same and a mug of joe for his little pal from the Pecos. He'd ordered in Spanish without thinking, seeing he was commencing to feel in Rome. But Miguelito laughed bitterly, and said, "I should have known. You understood every word we were saying about you the other night in that other town, no?"

To which Longarm could only reply in a modest tone, "*Comprendo poquito*. I can't say I agreed with either extreme view expressed about me. It was mean of you boys to take me for an honest piano player's pimp and I ain't half as dangerous as your short pal made me out to be. I'm just an old West-by-God-Virginia boy trying to get by as best he can in a world he never made and, like I said, I was never after anyone riding with you to begin with."

Miguelito stared thoughtfully down at the unexpected late-night snack Longarm had ordered for him as he asked, in that case, why they seemed to keep meeting up along the Ogallala Trail.

Longarm asked, "*Cómo cono lo quieres?* We're on a public right of way, *cabrón*! Where else should we keep meeting up, the middle of the Great Salt Lake? I got off the train at Kanorado to follow the damned trail north to this damned town. I had to pass through Rusty Springs to get here, the same as you all. So now it's your turn to tell me what you pests are doing this far north when no Texas cattle are due to start north this side of May Day."

Miguelito began a tedious explanation about scouting the new trail ahead of the market drive they were planning on for later that season. Longarm said, "Aw, shit, eat your supper. If I put this fool gun of mine away can I have your word we ain't at feud no more?"

The Tex-Mex grudgingly conceded, "If I have your word you will not do that to Junior Brown. How did you do that to me, *El Brazo Largo*?"

Longarm said, "I ought to keep it a trade secret, but seeing we're pals, now, nobody with a lick of sense gets in a quick-draw contest if he can possibly avoid it. Despite all that twaddle about me and some others in them eastern magazines about the West, we carry our side arms in holsters because we'd look silly walking around all day with our guns in our hands. But after that a gun in its holster ain't good for much shooting. So you have to get it out of your holster before you can shoot anybody with it, see?"

"Are you mocking me?" asked the *segundo*, stiffly.

Longarm replied, "I'm mocking Ned Buntline and Reporter Crawford of the *Post*, describing gunfights that would never take place betwixt serious gents who knew shit about guns. There *have* been times when I was caught by surprise and had to go for my holstered gun. I don't mind telling you such times are ass-puckering times indeed! So when I see trouble *coming*, I like to get my gun out from under my coattails and just hold it in my lap until the trouble gets to me. So do I look like the sort of asshole who'd sit in a lamp-lit beanery exposed to anybody passing in the darkness with my fucking gun in its fucking *holster*?"

Miguelito del Pecos laughed in a surprisingly boyish tone and said, "I shall have to remember such good advice, and these *huevos rancheros* are not bad, but I think I would have rather had them with *cerdo* or perhaps *pollo*, no?"

Longarm didn't comment. He knew that despite inventing the western beef industry as it had expanded since the war, Mexicans didn't enjoy beef half as much as pork or chicken. Down Mexico way they gave the remains of fighting bulls to the poor folk, who pissed and moaned because they were reduced to eating nothing but beef with their tortillas and beans.

By the time they were sharing three-for-a-nickel cheroots over coffee and dessert they'd both agreed they had surprisingly similar crosses to bear.

The *segundo* had to keep a spoiled only son from getting himself shot as a man by mistake and Longarm seemed to be looking for a man who was looking for the man who'd already shot a similar pain in the ass.

Miguelito rode for the Browns of Callahan County, well south of the combined Marner holdings. But he'd heard tell of the death of Cracker Marner and knew the Widows Marner by rep if not in the biblical sense. Longarm kept the thread of their conversation closer to Cracker Marner, his doting momma and adoring wife. They both agreed neither widow sounded all that rational.

After that there seemed to be a difference in style when anyone had pissed either one of the Widows Marner off. Knowing his own breed way better than some writing melodramas in English, Miguelito didn't find it odd how the Anglo-Saxon elder widow, Miss Melony, could bide her time for many a year and avenge the death of her man so long after he'd been killed by Indians. He didn't find it odd that the younger widow, Miss Dulcenia, was reputed to have a temper reserved in works of fiction for Scotch-Irish mule skinners with drinking problems.

Miguelito liked Miss Dulcenia best as the one who'd sent that hired gun under a Texas hat to track down and clean the plow of that earlier mystery man who'd gunned down Cracker Marner. He suggested Longarm worry more about the more recent killings—three, so far—because the killer still seemed to be hanging about Hardwater whilst that earlier rider on the blue roan hadn't been seen for six or eight months, anywhere along the Ogallala Trail.

Longarm blew a thoughtful smoke ring and decided, "I suspect they all came in by rail as far as Kanorado. They all hired livery mounts near the station and rode this far north with them for certain. Had the earlier one abandoned that distinctive blue roan to board another train somebody would have recovered it somewhere close to the trail."

Miguelito washed down the last of his chocolate cake, Mexicans being crazy for the chocolate their Indian predecessors had invented, and decided, "*Bueno*, in which case that one and his pretty *caballo* were far, far away by the time that second *buscadero* came looking for him just days ago. He must be most *stupido* as well as *muy malo*. They say Dulcenia Galvez y Cabrillo O'Brian Marner was thrown out of her convent school, despite the wealth and position of her people, for because she could not control her temper and often took offense at the wrong *muchacha*. I find it harder to picture an older woman who could wait . . . how many years?"

Longarm said, "Close to twenty. Cracker Marner lost his daddy to Comanche in his boyhood, whilst the Comanche were riding high across the Staked Plains. They were still Quill Indians whilst his momma managed to keep him out of a war the rest of us kids were invited to. But by '69, four years after Lee surrendered, the B.I.A. had the Comanche coming in to Fort Sill in the Indian Territory for some peace and quiet along with government handouts."

"Was then the older widow struck?" asked the Tex-Mex.

Longarm shook his head and said, "That would have made her revenge too easy. Her man had been run over by *serious* Comanche. So the war chief who'd lifted her husband's hair rode with Quanna Parker as a hold-out at the second battle of Adobe Walls as late as '74. Then, seeing the second battle of Adobe Walls killed more Comanche than Kit Carson killed in the first one, the last of the wild bunches came in by '76, just as the Lakota were acting up at Little Big Horn."

He drained his coffee mug and added, "By this time the war chief who'd counted coup in his salad days on the elder Marner must have been looking forward to a comfortable retirement in the frame house the B.I.A. provided for him and his wives, plural. Then, one summer evening in '77, there came a knock upon his doorstep and some person or persons unkown removed his name from the B.I.A. rolls. But I'm pretty sure he'd been known as Eyes-All-Over, and they say he'd been putting on weight eating B.I.A. rations."

Miguelito smiled sleepily and decided, "*Que linda*, they say revenge, like wine, improves with age. The *pobrecito* must have felt sure they would never make him pay for the fun he had growing up. But, tell me, would a woman who could wait a generation for to avenge the death a husband hire such a gun so *soon* for to avenge a son?"

Longarm pointed out, "Cracker was her *only* son, and she can't be getting any younger. But I follow your drift and a natural-born spitfire with hot-tempered kith and kin . . . Hold on, that may mean something."

Miguelito asked what and Longarm pointed out, "From all I've heard tell of the younger Widow Marner, she and her whole tribe are land-grant Spanish. You'd think she'd send a trusted retainer with a more Spanish manner about him if she was the one calling the tune up this way, wouldn't you?"

Miguelito dryly remarked, "I fit that picture better than your hawk-faced Anglo killer. Do you wish for me to confess in writing or will you take my word for it?"

Longarm smiled thinly and truthfully replied, "Already considered you and scratched you off as unlikely, no offense. You and your bunch would have been farther to the south than Rusty Springs, where we first met up, at the time that barkeep and government brand inspector were gunned down here in Hardwater last week."

Miguelito sighed, "*Ay, mierda*, I was looking forward to the fine cooking at your famous Leavenworth Prison and now I must ride on all the way to Nebraska with that *fregado* they have saddled us with!"

So they shook and parted friendlier than they'd met and Longarm strode back up Market Street to his hotel as hither and yon a streetlamp guttered out. For it was getting late and they didn't waste lamp oil on the owl birds in a small town on a tight budget.

As a seasoned traveler, Longarm had naturally held on to the room key they'd hired out to him. You could tell a tourist who'd stayed in few hotels before by the way they pestered the desk clerk with their infernal keys, not knowing he didn't give a shit where your fool key might be as long as you didn't owe for another day or try to sneak a second party into a single occupancy. So the night man dozing behind the desk never looked up as Longarm passed by in his well-broken-in, low-heeled army stove-pipes.

He made no noise on the stairs as he mounted them on the balls of his feet, unconscious of the Indian walk some of his friends and foes had commented on. He'd simply learned early on that in spite of the advantages of the high-heeled cowboy boot, it was a noisy son of a bitch and rough on the feet if you had to walk around a lot, as a lawman was more inclined to than your average trail herder.

Hence nobody behind any of the doors to either side heard him as he strode along the dimly lit hall corridor to the corner room he'd hired with cross-ventilation in mind. The poet who'd written that April was the cruelest month had been thinking about England's flukey spring weather, but his notion fit greenup time on the high plains better.

The light was dim indeed, but when a man was looking for a white match stem against a dark hall runner it was easy enough to spy.

So Longarm drew his .44-40 with his right fist and

gingerly tried the knob with his left. When he found the door unlocked he opened it sudden and whipped in to crab sideways along the wall, throwing down on the figure seated upright on the bedstead.

There was just enough light from outside to see it was shemale, seated with empty hands against the bedding to either side. So he didn't shoot her. He said, "Just stay put until we can have more light on the subject, ma'am."

As he seemed to belie himself, moving swiftly to shut the shutters and plunge the room into total darkness, the gal who'd been laying in wait for him there said, "I am Sally Arrowmaker. My brother, Bobby, has done a dumb thing. They told us you would be coming and I think I know who you really are. So hear me, I will do *anything*, anything you ask, if you can keep my poor younger brother from going to prison. He is Osage. Half Osage, anyway, and if they send him to prison he will die there, as so many others of the painted nations have, by his own hand if his heart does not break inside his chest!"

Longarm secured the last shutter as he calmly replied, "I'd been planning on paying you and your kid brother a call, Miss Sally. My shutting the shutters like this ain't meant disrespectsome. I mean to light the lamp. But I just hate it when somebody outside takes a potshot from the dark at me."

Suiting action to his words, Longarm thumbnailed a match head to light the reading lamp by the bedstead. As he did so he was treated to a vision of, say, twenty-odd with dusky cameo features framed by braided black hair that shone like raven wing feathers in the flattering lamplight, albeit her mighty trim figure seemed encased in the black-and-white outfit of a fashionable French maid.

As he shook out the match, Sally Arrowmaker said, "My brother told me about that man who killed somebody in the Boxelder Saloon last summer. The one who rode in on a . . . *shunkawakansota*, my brother told me in our own language. I am not sure how you say that in *Wasichu*."

"Blue roan would be close enough," Longarm decided, seeing Osage was close enough to the Lakota he knew somewhat better.

The beautiful Osage breed sprang to her feet to throw her arms around him as she smiled up at him adoringly to exclaim, "I was almost sure the lawman your people call Longarm had to be the one my people call *Wasichu Washstey*!"

Then she kissed him, right friendly, white-style.

So Longarm, being a natural man, kissed her back, French.

Chapter 7

She pulled away more like a white gal in a French maid's outfit than an Indian gal kissing French, saying, "Wait, we have to talk, first. Do I have your promise that you won't put my brother in prison if I let you put it in me?"

Longarm said, "You're right. We'd better talk, first. I just this evening read your brother's testimony at that coroner's inquest in the lobby downstairs. Are you saying he gave a false statement under oath?"

She shook her pretty head and sat back down as she explained, "He was never asked. So he never said. When I got off here at this hotel to cook supper at home he told me everything he knew, everything, including that first killer riding in on that . . . blue roan. The cruel *Wasichu* who killed our friend Luke told my brother he'd be back. If I tell you what Bobby told me about the man Luke's killer is hunting for, *he* might come back to Hardwater, too!"

Longarm soberly replied, "I'd be lying if I said it wasn't possible that second one's suspicions sound impossible, Miss Sally. Nobody ever saw hide nor hair of that distinctive pony the killer of Cracker Marner rode off on last summer. But the one somebody sent the second one after must have his reasons for suspecting the cuss never left this stretch of the Ogallala Trail."

As he tossed his hat aside and hung his frock coat on a handy hook the gal with at least some Indian lore to go with her grasp of their lingo asked, "How would that be possible? If he never rode far on the blue roan everyone remembers, why hasn't anyone ever seen it? Do you think he might have changed its color?"

Longarm chuckled at the picture and draped his gun belt over a bedpost to sit down beside her, saying, "I know another lady who surely never started out with henna-rinsed hair. But dipping an entire horse in hair dye sounds more complicated than just burying it in a hole, and let us not forget it was branded distinctive, Double Diamond X, registered under said brand as the property of a livery outfit just down the trail in Kanorado. So your brother's *shunkawakansota* works a couple or more ways. That first rider could have simply rid on off for keeps and the second killer could be barking up the wrong tree for a dumb reason. Or the man who rode off on the blue roan could have swapped with another rider who never brought it back, *or* the one and only mystery rider could have rode the blue roan to where he'd been headed in the first place and then come back, aboard another bronc entire, if he has any reason to linger in these parts."

"Why would he do that, after killing a man here and getting away clean?" she asked.

Longarm said, "I don't know. I *do* know that second killer suspects he has, and when you study on it, he must have had some reason for being in Hardwater the night he killed Cracker Marner. It was noted at the time he hadn't ridden in with any of the herds passing through and he'd have been remembered better if he'd been a resident all that long. So it figures he was new in town, at the time, leastways, with serious concerns on his mind. I wasn't there, but from the way the earlier inquest findings read, he was drinking alone in the Boxelder when Cracker Marner started up with him for no sensible reason and got his fool self shot without a word of discussion, for some reason his killer still knows better than us, unless you or your kid brother have been talking to him about his moody nature lately."

She repressed a shudder and murmured, "Our Lakota cousins have told us you read the wind better than a *matonagi*, I mean a spirit bear, but hear me, by *mitakuye oyasin*, all my people back to the beginning, my brother, Bobby, does not know and cannot name that rider of the blue roan who killed that *Wasichu* called Marner!"

Longarm nodded in sudden understanding and chose his words some before he replied, "I can see how a part-Osage stable hand might not care to gossip about even a strange *ilsey wichasha*. Did Bobby say whether the one who killed Cracker Marner was a breed or full-blood? Does Bobby know his nation?"

She sobbed, "I should never have come here! It is true! You have *pejuta*! *Pejuta tanka*! Nobody can hope to keep a secret from you! I think I want to go home now!"

Longarm gently but firmly shoved her on her back across the bedcovers as he said, "Hear me, *wichinchala*, I have not been sent to arrest the breed or full-blood who gunned Cracker Marner. I know that sounds *witko* but that's the way our laws work. The killing of that Texas trailboss, the barkeep across the way and even that stable hand last night don't add up to one federal offense. Are you still with us?"

She propped herself up on one elbow, the effect being much like those saloon paintings of Miss Cleopatra, save for her more modest attire, to reply, "I think so. Are you saying you don't care about my brother fibbing at the hearing they held downstairs this afternoon?"

Longarm smiled down at her to warn, "Let's not be sickening about it, *wichinchala*. To begin with, if they never asked him to describe the first rider that second rider was asking about, your brother never lied to them. In the second place, if he *had* covered up for a rider of his own complexion, that would be betwixt him, his conscience and the state of Colorado at this end of Market Street."

"*Washtey*, then he's not in trouble after all!" she chortled.

But Longarm told her, "The both of you could be in a whole lot of trouble. The first killer could be worried about Bobby telling tales out of school. The second killer could have seen by now he might have been questioning the wrong stable hand about that blue roan. So, for openers, do you all have a good yard dog, stout locks and at least one box of shotgun shells out at that spread of yours on the Kansas side of town?"

She told him she'd forted her kid brother up in her own basement rest and changing facilities, down below. So he drew back the hand he'd been fixing to slide closer as he said, "Smart move. Did you tell your brother you were coming up here to talk to me about your family troubles?"

She lay back, smiling up at him like Mona Lisa as she told him, "Of course not. He told me not to tell anybody else about that Osage full-blood riding a blue roan, and I wouldn't want Bobby to suspect I was fucking anybody just to keep him out of prison."

She'd already answered two questions he'd been about to press her about. So now he knew that first solitary drinker had been a moody, assimilated Osage, likely an out-of-work scout, now that all of the traditional enemies of the Osage Nation were hardly in the market for being scouted. As for any other matters they still might have to settle, a healthy man about recovered from Red Robin the night before had to consider more than one angle, smiling down at the temptations reclined across the covers beside him.

Everybody knew how white gals could be expected to respond to a friendly approach to some slap and tickle. They'd either cotton to the notion or they'd tell you right out they weren't that sort of gals. Either way, parting friendly was the hardest row to hoe.

Indian gals were neither more nor less inclined to screw than white gals. Some were. Some weren't. The main difference Longarm had noticed in his travels was that Indians were both more delicate and way less inclined to *tachesli* or bullshit around about natural needs or feelings. [They lived closer to the down-home earth, closer to the fire after sundown.] Plains nations, such as the Osage and their Comanche enemies were more open than whites with their flesh and less open about their feelings. Longarm had spent more than one evening in a tepee, agreeing with his gracious hosts not to notice one daughter of the house nursing a good-size kid whilst another tore off a piece under a buffalo robe with the boy from next door, and when a horse Indian felt the need to shit, he or she simply squatted and dropped it, politely, downwind of the camp and not too close to drinking water.

But Indians could be cautious about letting their true feelings show. They were inclined to laugh, lots more than white folk gave them credit for, and nobody could tell a dirty joke with more sly humor than Mister Lo. But letting on you were *serious* about something struck most Indians about the way it might have struck a Victorian family had a white boy announced at the supper table that he'd just learned to jack off and thought if felt swell to do so whilst peeking at his bare-ass momma through the keyhole.

Longarm had been there when an Indian youth had called a gal from her tepee with his nose flute, only to be told right out that the light of his life was having her period or would have as soon gone down on all fours for any disgusting cur dog. Indian gals didn't mess around, with good reason. Had a Quill Indian gal told anyone courting her that she liked him a lot but had to save it for some prince she expected to come along, she'd have been left to wait for her prince forever as a crazy woman it might not be good medicine to talk to.

But the question before the house in his hired hotel room that evening was whether Sally Arrowmaker felt like an Osage gal with some white blood or a white gal who was part Indian. For like most men, red or white, who knew what they wanted, Longarm's wants were tempered by not wanting to appear a brute, or, even worse, a fool.

Sally had kissed like a woman grown who knew her own mind, and it had been herself, not him, who'd come right out with that four-letter Anglo-Saxon verb. But on the other hand she was wearing high button shoes as well as a French maid's outfit and her Indian parted and braided hair smelled of violet pomade instead of sweet-grassed lard.

So Longarm was debating the advantages and disadvantages of an honest approach, knowing how few women really cottoned to that, no matter what they said, when Sally Arrowmaker sighed and softly asked him, "Why are you teasing me, *Wasichu Washtey*? Don't you think I am pretty? Don't you want *tawitan* with me, now that we have agreed my brother does not have to go to prison?"

That was a serious question.

Lest there be any confusion about it, later, Longarm gently but firmly warned her, "That ain't the deal, Miss Sally. I said I had no call to arrest your kid brother. I never said I won't, should ever I cut across anything federal to charge him with."

He could see he had her thinking. He told her, "Feel free to just be on your way with no harm done if that ain't good enough for you. I'm a natural man with natural feelings and I'd be trying to feed both a mess of *tachesli* if I said I didn't want you so bad I can taste it. But after that I'm packing a badge and I'm sworn to uphold the law."

"Didn't you say *federal* law?" she demurely asked, reaching for his questing hand to guide it where it had been wanting to go.

As they got it up under her black poplin skirt and linen apron Longarm felt obliged to warn, "I did. I said that as things now stood I was way more interested in the man who killed that government brand inspector than a local shooting six or eight months stale. But I might have to nose around about the man I'm after seems to be after, seeing that was his declared motives in both the saloon and the tack room where he gunned your brother's side-kick down. Do you reckon if we work together, we could get your brother to give us a better description of this Osage rider he seems to be covering for?"

As he discovered that, like heaps of Indian gals as well as good old sanitary Red Robin, this pretty breed had plucked or shaved her pubic hairs. He was trying to determine which as she calmly parted her thighs, confiding, "I can already describe the one who came back for his blue roan after shooting that trailboss in the saloon. Bobby was really upset at suppertime tonight. I know he wasn't holding anything back, from me, as he babbled in Osage about feeling so *Wasichu* at that hearing, trying not to let his feelings show as he just knew they were all convinced he was lying to them. Could you pet it with two fingers, please?"

He could and he did, as she calmly told him, "Bobby says that full-blood who rode off on the *shunkawakansota* was shorter and slimmer than him, and Bobby is not as big and husky as poor Luke Warner was. Bobby said the stranger never evoked *wolakota* as a member of the same nation, but replied in the language of our father when Bobby complimented him on his oddly colored pony. Bobby said the stranger looked thirty or forty. It is hard to tell with full-bloods, even for us. Bobby said they only spoke a few words in the lamplit stable after sundown, coming and going. But he thinks he would have remembered the stranger he had never seen before if the stranger had come back to Hardwater, as that second stranger must suspect."

Longarm asked if her brother had described any scars, limps or other unusual details. Sally sighed and said, "No! Don't you want to fuck me, now? As I told you, Bobby described a full-blood he'd only seen coming and going, last summer, as a short, slight Indian in dusty *Wasichu* trail clothes and, oh yes, a double-action pistol worn low and tied down. You men always seem more interested in things like that."

Longarm murmured, "It comes with the territory," and kissed her, French, as he drove two fingers deeper to inspire her clit with the web of his thumb as he commenced to shuck her duds without his having to ask her.

The man who'd been standing in the hall with his ear pressed to the door moved away in the dim light, smiling sly as a wolverine on its way out of a trapper's cabin, to slip down the back stairs and across the street to where a taller man armed with an army surplus Schofield was standing in the shadows under a burned-out streetlamp, gazing thoughtfully up at the lamplight glinting through the slats of Longarm's shutters.

As his shorter, white sidekick joined him, the hawk-faced killer Longarm was after quietly asked, "Well?"

The sneak who'd been lurking in the casually guarded

Majestic Hotel chortled, "Him and that Indian maid are fucking. They talked about you some before they got down to what they both really wanted. You'll be pleased to know they don't know shit. You and the boss lady were worried over nothing. That half-breed kid you should have shot instead has laid the killing of Cracker Marner, like we thought, on some mysterious gent he recalls as Osage. And so, in sum, the kid don't know shit, his big sister don't know shit and now Longarm don't know shit. So when do we ride, Frisco?"

The hawk-faced Frisco Harrigan, well known on many a wanted flier as a gun who rented by the hour, ran a thoughtful thumbnail through the stubble on his lantern jaw as he mused aloud, "Ain't certain. It might save us trouble, later, if we busted in up there right now and shot the both of them as they was fucking. Lord knows we'll never get a better crack at the rascal and he seems to have the boss lady worried shitless."

Chapter 8

By the time they'd shared a couple of cheroots and a lot more positions, Longarm had gotten to know Sally Arrowmaker in more than the biblical sense.

She and her kid brother had shared unusual but fairly happy childhoods with other army brats, red, white or in between, west of the big muddy at a dozen outposts she could recall, with fond memories of their Indian dad, an army scout topkick and fair but somewhat firmer mom, listed on the regimental rolls as a laundress and cleaning woman. Sally didn't have to explain how even the sweetest white moms tended to slap a fresh face now and again whilst a full-grown Indian man who'd strike a child for any reason would be ridiculed as a shit-kicking coward.

Longarm had discovered in visits to many an Indian camp that both ways resulted in much the same sort of kids. He'd heard the Chinese seldom chastised children, either, albeit Japanese were said to beat the shit out of their kids. Sally said, and Longarm found it easy to believe, the army brats she'd started out with had grown up good, bad and indifferent no matter how their red, white or mixed-blood elders had tried to reason with them.

Longarm had known to begin with how Sergeant Arrowmaker had been killed at Pea Ridge. Longarm had Cherokee pals who still bragged a heap about that fight. Sally elaborated on how their white outcast mom, not rating a Union widow's pension as the unofficial spouse of an Indian attached to the army as an employee, like a surgeon, for another example, had taken advantage of the Homestead Act of '62 to file on a quarter-section near the Colorado–Kansas line, not knowing they'd be running a federal cattle trail right past her dooryard not all that many years after she'd died.

By that time, of course, Sally had been a woman grown and brother, Bobby, had been old enough to get his own job. They'd soon noticed day wages in a brand-new trail town had sharing a hundred and sixty acres of marginal cropland with the grasshoppers and prairie dogs beat.

Sally said they'd sold off some of their proven claim as city lots at a handsome price they'd put in the bank. They still lived in the frame house they'd replaced their original soddy with. So even though she'd hidden her kid brother in the hotel basement down below Sally was concerned that jasper who'd gunned down Luke Warner might burn them out whilst nobody was out yonder on guard.

Longarm patted her bare shoulder as they snuggled against the headboard, soothing, "I doubt any real pro would bother. They say he might be riding with a pal. He said he was and they told me he was at that livery down in Kanorado. If so, it would be duck-soup simple for them to scout your place, see nobody was home, and ride on without betting that chip. Why take the chance of being spotted, raising hell with an empty house like mean little kids?"

She snuggled closer and confided she felt so much

safer, now that they'd become such pals. He absently slid his hand on that side from her bare shoulder down to one naked tit, marveling once again how a gal built so much slimmer across the hips could have bigger tits than the older and more rounded Red Robin.

Sally's bigger, tawny tits were firmer, too. He suspected her overall firmness was as much the result of her harder exercise than her Indian blood. But it was funny how even chunky Indian gals felt more solid than most white gals with that much meat on their bones.

He didn't mind one bit. One of the things he liked the best about womankind was that no matter how many of them you undressed, they most often surprised you some. And yet despite the fact that none of them were exactly the same, inside or out, most every one of them screwed just grand.

A man had to be a sport about the one out of ten who wasn't a great lay. Novelty was the spice of life and the very few who inspired a man to wonder what he'd ever seen in them could inspire him to really enjoy the next gal down the pike.

Since both Red Robin the night before and Sally Arrowsmith on this occasion were great in bed, and a man never knew when a winning streak would peter out, he snubbed out their smoke and put that hand in her lap, glad that they'd both shaved or plucked their old ring-dang-doos bare and savoring the slight differences of their basic equipment as he confided, "There's something else I've been meaning to ask you. You'd know as much about it as Marshal Breen and it could save my having to pestering him about it."

Sally brought her knees up and spread them apart as she demanded, "What are you talking about? You don't want that old man to suck it for you, do you?"

He confessed the thought had never crossed his mind,

but asked if Marshal Breen or any of the other town lawmen had reps for queer beliefs.

She said, "Not that I know of. But why go to strangers when you have a friend like me? Just lay back and let me smoke your *canunpa* for you, my *tatanka witko*!"

He started to say that hadn't been what he'd wanted to ask her. Then he wondered why any man with a lick of sense and half an erection would want to say a dumb thing like that. So a grand time was had by all as she smoked the pipe of her mad bull whilst he strummed her old banjo with his *napey*, as she called his hand every time she grabbed hold of his wrist to move it faster.

They finished right, old-fashioned for a change, and then he got to tell her he'd really meant to inquire about other small holdings out around the town of Hardwater.

He explained, "Tracking across open range ought to be fairly easy, this time of the year, and everybody seems to feel they're trying to cut the sign of two strange horses."

She didn't ask how good trackers distinguished the work of local blacksmiths from others. She was an army brat and even townie gals had read how easy it had been for a posse of Minnesota farmers to cut the trail of the James-Younger gang's out-of-town hoofprints.

Longarm used that bunch by way of illustration when he told her, "We know way more about Frank and Jesse since the Miller boys were killed and the Younger boys were captured after that Northfield raid blew up in their faces. It used to be thought they were magicians mounted on flying horses at the very least. But in point of fact their disappearing acts within a day's ride of Liberty, Missouri, were duck-soup simple. They had most all the smallholding trash-whites in Clay County fibbing for them. It's tough to stay on the trail of a gang tearing along a public right-of-way when grinning kids along the fence lines point the wrong way and tell you they just went around yonder corner."

Sally asked, "Then you suspect someone close to town might be sheltering the killer who murdered Gus Henson, Will Chambers and poor Luke Warner?"

Longarm kissed the part in her sweet-scented hair as he nodded and said, "The first two killings were last week. He shot Luke Warner and scared your brother a bare twenty-four hours ago. Had he and at least one pal been camping out on the lone prairie all this time, they'd have had to leave some sign. Even when you forego a campfire of cow chips, your ponies drop apples and your bedrolls flatten fresh sprouted shortgrass. I'd believe your Marshal Breen and his boys were queers before I'd buy them failing to cut sign off the trampled cattle trail or a campsite smack alongside it. So at least one and mayhaps two or three strange riders have been sticking to the beaten paths in and out of town, holing up somewheres safe between times."

Sally protested, "How could anyone get away with that, close enough to town to matter? There aren't three hundred families within a dozen miles and we all know one another!"

Longarm snuggled her closer as he said, "You mean you know one another well enough to howdy. It's been my experience as a lawman that all sorts of things can go on just inside lace curtains fronting on a city street, with nobody ever knowing unless somebody inside calls the law. Your *Wakan Tanka* only knows how many daughters or even mothers *satisfied* with incest never tell on dear old Dad or that sweet young man who's so good to his mother. Folk live ankle-deep in cockroaches and leave Mother to rot away in her bed because she told them not to disturb her rest. Others build sea-going vessels in their front parlors or fashion bombs on their kitchen tables and, again, nobody knows unless and until something *happens*. We only *hear* about the odd things some folks do behind closed doors when something goes wrong. So Frank and Jesse, according to one of the Younger boys who came down with the lung rot, were just hiding out with kith and kin a few paces off the road as the average posse thundered by. They never had any secret caves or tree houses. You mark my words, and when we catch up with them, we'll find Frank or Jesse resting up betwixt jobs in comfortable quarters, eating three square meals a day and bedding down at night with their ladies fair. That's how come the Pinkertons keep missing them, peering into mine shafts and abandoned farmhouses. Strange faces don't stand out in a crowd half as much as they might on open range or a transient hotel such as this one. So I'm betting on a nearby butter-and-egg spread, a hog farm or whatever."

Sally asked, "But what if somebody were to come to the door whilst your Frank and Jesse were having supper?"

He shrugged his bare shoulder under her reclining head and asked, "What if somebody did? How long does it take to rise from the table and step into a back room whilst one's gracious host or hostess takes some time answering the door? *I* can't push my way into anyone's house without a search warrant and I'm the *law*. How tough would it be to just hand over the cup of sugar your neighbor came to borrow and tell her you'd invite her in if only you didn't suspect you might be coming down with something catching. You're a woman who keeps house, *wichinchala*, so why am I telling *you* all this?"

She chuckled and said, "I suppose I could keep you a secret if I was having *tawiton* with you out at our place and Bobby wasn't home. But what was that you said about *three* possible strangers hiding out close to town like that? I thought you said they thought there might be two."

Longarm said, "That full-blood who gunned down Cracker Marner and the two sent after him add up to three. That first killer might not have ridden far, or if he did he might have come back. He must have been in town that night for some good reason. From the way it reads he might have been waiting to meet somebody there in the Boxwelder when the liquored-up Cracker Marner started up with him. The results were short and bitter out of all proportion to the blitherings of a fool. So that rider who'd left a blue roan in your brother's keeping must have been tensed up like a cornered sidewinder and he likely struck without taking time to study on it. Then, once he had, he ducked over to the Municipal Corral to mount up and ride, near or far, as long as it was out of sight."

He kissed the part of her hair some more and added, "Somebody you likely know must have been sheltering him all the while or since his return. Either way, there has to be something close at hand that he's still interested in. So that's one answer worth looking for. The other most logical question would be who spotted him close to town and told whoever's sent those other killers to clean his plow. Let's start as close to town as we can. Might you and your brother know many others of the Osage or simply *ilcey wichasha* persuasion, close enough to town to matter?"

She said, "No full-bloods. Some breeds, like Bobby and me, living off the B.I.A. rolls as full citizens. I know some breeds crawl on to the blanket because they lack the brains or the courage to take care of themselves. Bobby and me feel pity for such *ptehinchalan*. They are babies crying for *minipeta* to drown their shame!"

Longarm said, "I know how self-supporting breeds and full-bloods feel about wards of the government. There's a bakery in my part of Denver owned and operated by full-blood Arapaho and one of the other deputies I ride with is half Pawnee. So let's talk about assimilates like yourself and your kid brother, owning private property an easy lope down the Owlhoot Trail."

She started to reel off a list of names that sounded mostly white, since, unlike Cherokee, Pawnee and other Iroquoian speakers, most Plains nations traced their ancestry from their father's side, and white men taking up with Indian women was most common.

Longarm said he wanted to write the names down. Sally laughed when he sat up to fish his notebook from the vest that had somehow wound up on the floor. She said he had a pretty ass and kissed it to prove her contention.

So with one thing leading to another he just hung on to his notebook a spell until he could get her back in a dog-style position.

Once he had, his feet braced wide on the rug and the notebook and pencil stub in hand, he gravely asked her to go over those local addresses some more as he moved in and out of her.

He'd long since assumed she had to be experienced. She proved it by laughing and allowing, "This does seem a more comfortable position for conversation. But don't you dare slow down on me just to cross a *T* or dot an *I*!"

He thrust deep and promised he'd never, as long as she didn't lose the thread of their conversation just because they were coming.

So by the time they were, and he just tossed the blamed book to the four winds to grab hold of her sweet, swiveling hips, she'd given him thirteen places to call on, in and about Hardwater Township. Then, once they'd come and he'd lit another smoke for them, Sally asked him, "What if that Osage my brother didn't want to talk about could be hiding out with some *Wasichu* family you don't have on that list?"

To which Longarm could only reply, snorting smoke out both nostrils like a *tatanka witko* indeed, "I reckon I'll just have to search for him somewhere else. Like I told you. I ain't out to arrest him on a local charge. I just want somebody to tell me who those rascals who came here to kill him might be."

She smiled and decided, "In that case I may have done that Osage a favor in coming to you."

Longarm chuckled fondly and confided, "You sure did me a favor, coming *with* me, all those times."

Chapter 9

Come morning, Longarm broke fast on tolerable flapjacks and pork sausages with a side order of a Denver omelet in the hotel dining room off the lobby. The waitress looked as if she'd had a good screwing the night before as well, in spite of her flat chest and hair the color of that fuzz that collects under the bed.

As he was leaving, Sally was coming up from the basement in a fresh French outfit to start her day job, looking as if butter wouldn't have melted in her mouth. Longarm ticked his hat brim to her, she nodded shyly and they passed as if that was the size of it. If the room clerk knew anything he sure played poker good.

Longarm went first to the Western Union near the intersection of east-west Market Street and the wider north-south narrowing of the cattle trail through town. Seeing Billy Vail had sent him there, he asked if they had any wires for him. They had one. Knowing how Billy hated to waste wired words at a nickel a throw, Longarm opened the sealed yellow envelope before he composed his own progress report. Vail's wire read, "IF YOU NOT THERE YET WHY NOT QUESTION MARK BE ON LOOKOUT FOR FRICO

HARRIGAN AND PUD BARKER COMMA TALL AND LEAN
SHORT AND HUSKY SPOTTED BY PINKERTONS GETTING OFF
AT KANORADO LAST WEEK STOP TIME AND REPS AS HIRED
GUNS FITS STOP BE CAREFUL, STOP VAIL."

Longarm's return message covered the little he knew
so far and asked his home office to look into Miguelito
del Pecos and the Browns of Callahan County, Texas.
Then he sent another wire to a pal with the B.I.A. at the
Fort Sill Comanche Reserve.

Leaving the Western Union, he was met by that kid
deputy from the night before and an older skinny cuss
dressed like an undertaker but introducing himself as the
town law, Marshal Breen. They shook on that and strode
together to the Boxelder Saloon for some sit-down suds
and a view of the scene of some crimes as they brought
one another up to date.

The kid deputy went on about his own beeswax as the
two older lawmen took the same corner table Brand Inspector Will Chambers had been sitting at the evening of
his recent death. Breen didn't have to explain how at least
one saloon in every cow town was open around the clock.
But he did tell Longarm the Greek kid taking their orders
had been off the evening Chambers and the night man
had been shot.

When he added the Greek hadn't been working there
at all when that short, dark stranger had gunned that Texican, Longarm idly asked how you could tell a Greek
from, say, Black Irish.

That had been a test. Breen passed it by wearily replying, "There you go with that same mistake about my kin.
It all happened before my time. But whilst it's true the
Black Irish and the Orange Irish can't get along in the old
country, the Black Irish are the Catholics and the Orange
Irish are the Protestants. That dark brunette Irish type you
sometimes see hail mostly from the western counties and

75

just sprout that way whichever church they go to. Some say they're left over from the little people who got to Ireland before the Celts. I've heard it said shipwrecked Spaniards from that lost armada might account for such dago-looking Harps. My father's people were from Waterford and my mother's people were Dutch, so I don't care."

He sipped some suds before adding, "As for how you tell a Greek from one of the little people, you ask. It's my job to ask newcomers to Hardwater who they might be. Spyros, yonder, is one of the two brothers Macropolis. His elder brother would be Stavros. Raises pigs and chickens downwind of town on the Kansas side of the line. Stavros bought the Callas spread last September and when Spyros came out to join them he took this town job to bring in some ready cash whilst they wait to show a decent profit on the old Callas place."

"Ain't Callas a Greek name, too?" asked Longarm casually as he got out some smokes.

Breen said, "It must be. Nick Callas was another Greek who gave up his barely proven claim for enough to move on out California way. His wife, another Greek, allowed the winters in these parts got into her bones before Halloween and they didn't thaw out before the Fourth of July. Old Stavros Macropolis don't have to worry about his own wife nagging him about our climate. He married up with a squaw. *Said* he married up with her, leastways. You never ask a man to show you a wedding certificate without just cause to suspect abduction or statutory rape and his old woman must be thirty if she's a day."

"Do you know her nation?" asked Longarm, having already heard how Osage stuck together.

Breen said, "Sure I do. I told you I'm supposed to. Miss Alice Macropolis would be Cherokee. I understand Stavros married her down at Fort Smith. I've never asked him what he was doing in Fort Smith before he came up this way to buy the Callas place. I ain't paid to police any part of Arkansas. What do you suspect Macropolis and his Cherokee squaw of, Longarm?"

So Longarm had to tell him he had reason to believe that earlier dark stranger who'd gunned down Cracker Marner, over by that very bar, had likely been an assimilated Indian, dressed cow and on some serious beeswax that had tensed him up past common sense.

Breen nodded thoughtfully and said, "Swatting a mean drunk like a fly ain't sensible unless you have to. But what do you reckon he was up to, here in Hardwater, and who told you he was an Indian?"

Longarm said, truthfully enough when you studied on it, "I only heard that part as secondhand gossip. I've yet to canvas anybody I could ask for a more detailed description. As for why he was here or mayhaps passing through, it's too early to say."

It didn't work. Breen was worth whatever they were paying him to police their dinky trail town. He insisted, "Who told you he might have been an Indian? I asked high and I asked low at the time of the shooting late last summer and nobody hereabouts told me shit about him being more than a fleet dark shadow!"

Longarm said, "I just wired the Bureau of Indian Affairs about an earlier incident in the noisy life of the late Cracker Marner. They say his daddy was killed by an Indian and his momma might have hired somebody to track down the guilty Comanche war chief and kill him on the reservation he'd settled down on. He was gunned down on his own doorstep, in the middle of the Comanche reserve, and nobody recalls a white stranger riding in or out at supper time, when you'd expect a white stranger to be noticed. So I suspect that hired gun must have looked as if he belonged there, coming and going."

He got their two cheroots going and shook out the match as he went on, "Cracker Marner was just a kid when his dad was killed, but old enough to dodge the Dixie draft before his upset momma hired some Indian wearing a Texas hat and a low slung six-gun. So what if Cracker had been in on avenging his father's death? Going over the depositions you took yourself last summer, Cracker Marner came in here liquored up, spotted a lone stranger in a far corner and went whooping over to call him his long-lost bastard. Are you with me so far?"

Breen nodded soberly and said, "They told us you were good. You're saying a boisterous asshole recognized a hired gun who didn't want it bruted about that he was this far north of Texas. Shooting suddenly, before his victim could spill any more beans, works better than some homicidal maniac who prefers to drink alone. But let's say you have a sensible motive and a better description for that killer, what in thunder was he doing here in Hardwater? Ain't nobody else been shot betwixt the murder of Cracker Marner last year and them three more recent killings."

Longarm said, "I know. I was hoping I could concentrate on just the federal offense against Will Chambers. But it's commencing to look as if he was an almost innocent bystander caught in the cross fire of a fucking local affair we're just going to have to claim for Uncle Sam!"

The local lawman grinned like a mean little kid and said, "Hot damn! Where do we start?"

It was a good question. Longarm sighed and said, "All over Robin Hood's barn, from the headwaters of the Brazos to here, with Fort Sill along the way. So now I have to send more telegrams and I have the blamed reports I need in my saddlebag at the hotel."

Marshal Breen volunteered to tag along and insisted on paying young Spyros himself. As they stepped outside

Longarm fished out his notebook to ask where that Callas place the new Greek bunch had bought might be.

Breen said, "I told you. Downwind. You ride southeast out of town and cross the old Muller place, which now resembles a quarter-section of trampled dirt, campfire ash and trash-pit mounds. Jeb Muller gave up years ago after fucking up a hundred and sixty acres with a John Deere plow and an optimistic attitude about sweet corn and our summer rains. The scalped spread has been used ever since as a free campground and, yes, two trail outfits were bedded down with herds milled north and south the night your mysterious Indian gunned down the boss of one such outfit. Nobody told us an Indian on a blue roan hid out for the night on the old Muller spread and we scouted it for fresh sign right after that shooting last week and just this morning. Do you want a detailed list of every rabbit turd and tumbleweed we turned over?"

Longarm shook his head but said, "I'll have a look on my way out to canvas Greek Stavros and his Cherokee wife."

Before Marshal Breen could answer a rifle spanged, high but not too far away, and both lawmen dove behind the same watering trough as the rifle spanged a second time, showering their hats with warm, stagnated water.

Breen grunted, "Rooftop, across the way!" in a stagnant tone.

So Longarm said, "I see the smoke. They came from ahint that false front above the hardware. How bad are you hit?"

The older lawman wheezed, "Bad enough. Go *git* him, pard!"

So Longarm tried and that was easier said than done. He'd had no idea Market Street was really that wide before he'd run across it, zigzagging from side to side, as somewhere ahead of him more shots rang out. And then he was inside a narrow hardware store, befogged with swirling gun smoke. But as he threw down on the only movement ahead of him, it called out, "Don't shoot! I'm with you! Heard the son of a bitch atop my roof. Saw poor Marshal Breen go down across the way. Emptied this new Winchester up through the ceiling. Fifteen rounds without one jam and ain't that something?"

Longarm replied, "Nice going. How do I get up there for a look-see?"

The hardware man led him back through the swirling gun smoke and out the back door, where a ladder built flush to the siding near the rear door led on up to the flat roof.

Longarm took a deep breath and said, "Cover me. I got to go up."

The hardware man warned, "If he's still up yonder, and still alive, you're fixing to get your head blown off, mister!"

To which Longarm could only reply, "I ain't a mister. I'm the law. And I never said I *wanted* to go up. I only said I *had* to."

Then he went on up and, when nobody blew his head off, he found four spent shell casings and a tarpaper roof in serious need of a patch job before the next spring rain. So that fusillade from below had chased the rooftop sniper off the roof before he could nail a running man crossing Market Street.

Longarm went back down to holster his .44-40 and break out his notebook as he gravely told the anxious hardware man, "You might have just saved my bacon and I'm putting that down in my final report. So could I have your name for the record, sir?"

The helpful hardware man described himself as one Amory Steiner. Longarm excused himself to dash back to where he'd left Marshal Breen behind that watering trough.

Breen was still there, but he wasn't alone. That kid deputy, Tim Colson, was there with the town-doc-cum-deputy-coroner, who'd torn Breen's shirt open after popping some vest buttons to get at the bullet hole in the older lawman's chest. Longarm could see it wasn't bleeding enough for a heart shot and Breen's breathing sounded less strained, now, as he asked Longarm how they'd done across the way.

Longarm said, "He got away, for now. We might find a witness if we canvas up and down the back alley. I just wrote your Amory Steiner for an assist. He chased the bastard off the roof and down the back ladder shooting up from down below."

Breen muttered, "Old Steiner is all right, for a Jew boy." Then he glanced up at his deputy to ask, "What are you waiting for, a pat on the ass? You heard the man say we wanted to canvas up and down that alley and the doc here has no more use for you than the rest of us."

So Tim Colson jumped to his feet and ran across to the open door of Steiner's hardware as Breen decided, "Tim's a good kid, for a Donegal man. If anybody spied the shit who shot me Tim will find them. How bad is it, Doc?"

The town-doc-cum-deputy-coroner said, "I am pleased to report I won't have to empanel a jury for this shooting, but it was close, Pete, close as hell. Your guardian angel must have been riding on that rifle round to steer it clean through you without hitting a major artery or vital organ."

Breen said, "Then help me to my damned feet so's I can track down the son of a bitch who just tried to kill me!"

The older medical man told him, "I'll do no such thing and you're not going anyplace before Greek Spyros gets back with the help I sent him for. I said you're going to live. But I told you how close it was, first. When the help from my clinic gets here we're going to scrub you down with carbolic soap and bed you down in boiled surgical linen. There's no telling where that bullet had been before it went all the way through you and I'll never speak to you again if you die on me from a mortified wound!"

"I can't stay laid up that long!" the town law protested, "I got to go after that son of a bitch who shot me, just now!"

But as he struggled with his old pal Longarm said, "Take it easy and do as he says. We won't know for at least seventy-two hours whether you have an infection or not and I'm still up and about to help Tim track him down."

Breen pouted, "It ain't fair. I was the one he was trying to kill. He was never aiming at you!"

Longarm didn't answer. He'd been raised to be respectful to his elders and it was *possible* the bullet through the town law had been meant for him instead of bigger game.

Chapter 10

The Greek barkeep came back with a short old goat and a big, Dutch-looking gal holding either end of a stretcher. The strapping blond filled her white linen uniform too tightly but not unsightly as Longarm helped them get the wounded Breen aboard to tote him to their clinic just west of the hotel. Then, seeing they'd be fussing over him a spell, Longarm went first to the town lockup, where Tim Colson had just lit up at the desk after finding not a soul who'd seen any stranger running through that alley behind Steiner's hardware.

When Longarm asked who else they might have seen, the junior deputy shrugged and said, "Most everybody. You can't blaze away from a rooftop in broad daylight without others coming out their back doors for a look-see. But none of the ones I talked to spied any stranger with a rifle."

"If it was a rifle." Longarm mused, patting his holster as he pointed out, "I load both my six-gun and my Winchester '73 with the same .44-40 rounds. I wasn't the first to notice you could do so, neither. So how do you like someone who didn't look so strange, just walking off, innocent, after peppering and reloading a concealed weapon atop Steiner's hardware?"

Colson said that had an invisible man beat, but asked, "Why would anyone who belongs here in Hardwater peg a shot at poor old Pete Breen? He has his faults, I will allow, but this is an election year. So who'd be *that* anxious?"

Longarm modestly suggested, "They might not have been aiming at him. I just got here and nobody gets to vote against me, come November. But I ain't likely to get the true story jawing here with you as time goes by, no offense. So I'm off to do some canvasing of my own."

He went back to his hotel for some papers he'd left in that saddlebag and picked up his Winchester whilst he was at it. In the hall he met up with Sally Arrowmaker and a feather duster. So he kissed her. But when she suggested they duck back inside for a quickie he pointed out that they were both on duty. So she called him a cold-hearted *yuwipi* and warned him she'd catch up with him later, leaving him to wonder what in thunder a *yuwipi* might be as he headed on for the Municipal Corral and Livery Services.

Longarm didn't claim to speak any Indian dialect fluent. He doubted any white man could follow the twists of the NaDéné lingo shared by the so-called Apache and Navaho. But he'd picked up dribs and drabs of the different high plains lingos and they all had grammars not too different from, say, Border Mex.

That wasn't to say *any* Indians talked in the cigar-store grunts of white playwrights, bless their uninspired imaginations. There *wasn't* any "Indian language" understood by Mister Lo and all his children. When they wanted to describe that uncertain mystery white writers translated best as "medicine" an Arapaho called it *matou*, a Comanche called it *puha* and a Lakota, or Osage, said *wakan*.

Yet all three shared simular notions about medicine and strung their words together in a way that made some college professors think they might have started out with the same lingo, long ago, like them Aryan folk who'd spoke the ancient lingo English, French and even Hindu seemed to have come down from.

As he strode along with his saddlebags and rifle, Longarm managed to recall that *yuwipi* was the Lakota, or Osage, for "stone." She'd have said he was *chan* if she'd thought him warm as a wooden Indian. So he had to laugh. It was too early in the morning to worry about the Osage for hot pepper.

At the livery the owner, the same iron-mustached bird he'd talked with before, had heard about the latest gunplay down the street and told Longarm he was ahead of him.

He said, "Nobody came running to saddle up and ride, Deputy Long. They must have tethered their mounts somewheres else."

Longarm said, "I mean to ride that chestnut barb I left with you out back, this morning. But since we're on the subject, might you recall a blue roan left in your keeping last summer, about the time of that other shooting in the Boxelder?"

The older man sighed and replied, "You're asking me to remember a *horse*, one horse, left with us six or eight months ago? What did you think we hired out, boarded, watered and fed, day after day by the dozens around here, bunny rabbits? How the hell would any of us remember a roan of any shade we might have cared for that far back? When you say blue roan you're talking about a pony with white guard hairs over black underfur, like you see on a silver fox, right?"

Longarm said that was about the size of it and felt no call to say Bobby Arrowmaker had recalled just such a pony out back. Longarm had promised his sister he wouldn't unless he had to.

As they went back to saddle and bridle the chestnut barb, Longarm asked about the buckskin and cordovan ponies missing from the same livery down Kanorado way. He pointed out, "Those two strangers would have ridden in less than a full seven days ago and they must have left their mounts with somebody. The one who gunned down the barkeep, a federal employee and your own Luke Warner was on foot as he shot all three."

The liveryman said, flatly, "Nobody left such stock with us. So what if the one killer moved in at dusk on foot whilst his sidekick held his pony for him just outside of sight?"

"To ride where?" Longarm demanded, cinching his army McClellan with a knee against the retired cow pony's ribs, knowing the hard way about your average cow pony's sense of fun.

As he dropped his Winchester in its saddle boot he elaborated, "After you shoot somebody and ride out of town you *ride* somewheres. You don't shinny up a moonbeam and haul your pony after you."

The local man soberly replied, "I know the boys failed to cut any sign. I rode with them when Gus Henson was shot last week. As near as we could read it, they stuck to the beaten path, never leaving the north-south cattle trail or the farm roads leading off from the same, not far enough to matter. I, for one, don't think they ever lit out across open range. They could have made her down to Rusty Springs and beyond before sunup, easy, sticking to the beaten path of that Ogallala Trail, couldn't they?"

Longarm said, "Mebbe. That's sure a lot of commuting back and forth betwixt two killings here in Hardwater. But like the old song has it, further along, we'll know more about it, Lord willing and the creeks don't rise."

Then, the helpful liveryman having bridled the barb, Longarm gathered the reins with a nod of thanks, mounted up and rode.

He rode first for that poultry and pig operation of the Brothers Macropolis, hoping to nail more than one bird with one *yuwipi*.

As he crossed the plow-scalped and tamped-down expanse set aside as a campground, now, he saw no fresh ashes or scuffed up 'dobe, as the solid clay under the unplowed sod of the high plains could be and was described by the kids of Denver, having 'dobe fights in the vacant lots of the same. By the Fourth of July the already crusty 'dobe would be set hard as wall plaster. But as yet it was willing to record hoof marks, Longarm saw, as he rode off the path for a look back at the trail his own mount was leaving across the overgrown vacant lot.

He rode on, wishing the wind would blow the other way as he and his mount caught their first whiffs of pig and chicken shit. A heap of pig and chicken shit. His pony balked at moving closer. Longarm heeled it sternly and said, "Oh, yes, we are, old gal. I'd prefer the more delicate perfume of cow shit or even horse shit, my own self, but we have us some chores to perform."

So they rode on in to the cluster of sod, tar paper and sun-bleached confusion around a trampled dooryard as chickens squawked and hogs squealed and grunted all around.

As he dismounted near the veranda of the long, low main dwelling with a tin roof and walls of sod, the top of a Dutch door opened to reveal the top half of a plain but pleasantly smiling Indian woman in a blue polka-dot housedress. She called out, "I'm sorry. I can't invite you in for coffee and cake because I'm here alone."

Longarm tethered his mount to a veranda pole as he explained how he was the law instead of a grub-line rider.

The woman of around forty, give or take a few years raising pigs and chickens, said, "You still can't come in. I know you may find this hard to believe, me being Cherokee and all, but my man is jealous as all get out and I'd rather have you think me rude than risk his thinking . . . what he's inclined to think whenever he catched me alone with a man."

Longarm said, "In that case I'll just talk to you from out here, ma'am, but talk we must. For I need some answers. Is it safe to assume this would be the Macropolis spread, and that you'd be the lady of the house?"

She said, "I'm Alice Macropolis. I used to be Alice Blackdrink down to Fort Smith until my Staffy made me his wedded wife."

She stared at him soberly and added, "His lawfully wedded wife. Recorded as such off the reservation by Sebastian County. You can look that up if you care to."

"I'll take your word for it," Longarm lied, explaining, "I ain't here to pester you or your man about your own affairs, Miss Alice. I was taken by the fact you seem to be of the Indian persuasion."

She snapped, "Three-quarters Indian, one-quarter Scotch-Irish and no nigger that I know of! What's it to you?"

He soothed, "I just said I wasn't here to pester anybody, Miss Alice. I'm here with the greatest respect, seeking the opinion of one assimilated Indian about another."

She told him to keep talking, as if interested despite herself.

So Longarm explained his suspicions about that mysterious rider on the missing blue roan, described by yet another local Indian as an Osage full-blood. When Alice Macropolis said she'd heard tell of the Arrowmaker kids but didn't know them well enough to offer an opinion, Longarm said, "I reckon I know them well enough, ma'am. What I'd like to know is this. Do you think an Osage, brought up to speak Osage, could pass for Comanche long enough to ride on and off a Comanche reserve one time?"

The Cherokee woman thought, shrugged and decided, "Why not, if he knew a few words of Comanche and didn't get into a religious argument with anybody? You say he was just riding through, that one time?"

Longarm nodded soberly and confided, "That's about the way I expected you to see it, ma'am. You wouldn't have to be a paid-up citizen of Old Mexico so, say, *buenoches* from under a shady hat brim as you rode through a border town late at night. So an Osage enemy acting friendly in passing could likely get in and out that one time. Then, later, meeting up with a white boy who knew he'd been paid to gun a retired Comanche . . . Yep, that works pretty good."

She leaned farther out over her door half, stretching her thin calico tighter over surprisingly firm cupcakes for such a hungry-looking old gal as she asked him to go on, explaining she had no idea what he was talking about.

He sighed and said, "I reckon I was talking mostly to myself, Miss Alice. The entire twisted tale gets tedious with the retelling. So suffice it to say I fear the same spiteful widow who hired that one Indian to gun down another has hired one or more white boys to track him down and pay him back for gunning down her spoiled brat!"

She opened her Dutch door all the way, saying, "You's better come in for some coffee and cake after all. I know I'm never going to get any sleep tonight unless you tell me the whole story!"

But before Longarm could take her up on her kind offer they both turned to the sound of thundering hoofbeats to see a big man on a small pony coming fast and furious.

Alice Macropolis said, "Aw, shit, that's my husband, Staffy. So don't say a word and let me do the talking!"

Longarm did. As the lathered Greek alit from his panting pony to join them, his Indian wife pleaded, "Before you say a word, Staffy, it's all right! This gentleman is a federal deputy and he's looking for some Osage outlaw, not anybody we know. I was just now fixing to invite him in for coffee and cake. Why don't you just tether your old Socrates for now and come inside with us?"

Stavros Macropolis said, "I was at the post office, asking about that mail-order windmill we ordered. We need more water out here, damn it!"

Longarm assured him the federal government wasn't interested in where he'd just been on his own time. He said, "I'm out here canvasing everyone in these parts about that recent gunplay in town."

As he followed them on in the bewildered Greek, who seemed to have been raised American, replied, "I figured somebody might. But how did you ever beat me out here? The shooting just happened minutes ago and I rode for home to guard my woman the moment I heard about it. For nobody's safe around Hardwater with that mad-dog killer on the loose!"

As the lady of the house moved over to her stove Longarm turned with a puzzled frown to demand, "Hold on. Are we talking about yet another shooting? A *sixth* shooting, since Marshal Breen was shot no more than two hours ago?"

Macropolis nodded his bushy head to reply, "This time he shot a kid. That breed stable boy, Bobby Arrowmaker. His sister found him bleeding in the basement at the Majestic Hotel when she went downstairs for some pine oil. They've taken the poor kid to the clinic, along with Marshal Breen."

Longarm was already in motion as the Greek added,

"They think the marshal's going to make it. But they don't hold out much hope for the Arrowmaker kid!"

Longarm didn't take the time to shout back more than an all-purpose adios as he untethered the chestnut and mounted up to ride, his mind in a whirl as he decided, at full gallop, "Aw, bird turds, no matter how you slice it, this don't make a lick of sense!"

Chapter 11

It lay just past noon by the time Longarm dismounted out front of the doc's combined clinic and residence, a three-story, Mansart-roofed pile of whitewashed frame with living quarters above and the clinic taking up what would have been the parlor floor of a larger family. Inside, they told Longarm they'd just carried Bobby Arrowmaker to the undertaker's. So he rode there next.

Like most everybody else in a town that size, their undertaker doubled in brass as the town's druggist and postmaster, with the post office to the rear of the drugstore and the undertaking down below. He found Sally Arrowmaker seated in the viewing chapel near the stairs with that strapping nurse from the clinic. The big blond was sort of holding the smaller breed gal in the French maid's outfit like a lost kid. She quietly told him they were working on the boy in the back.

Longarm sat beside them on the same sofa, with Sally betwixt them as he gently took one of her hands to murmur, "I don't know what to say, Miss Sally. Is there anything I can *do*?"

The petite brunette sounded surprisingly conversational

as she told him, "He was lying in the boiler room near the delivery stairs. He was trying to make it outside for some air when he collapsed. His lungs were full of blood and he'd coughed it up all over the cement floor. But he knew who I was and he said he was sorry. I told him he had nothing to be sorry about and asked him what had happened. He said that same one who'd shot Luke Warner had come down to the basement after him. That's all I heard. I ran upstairs for help. By the time we got back down to him he'd passed out. We never got to speak to one another again. And now I have no *mitakuye oyasin*! Now I am all alone from where the sun now stands, forever!"

"You've still got us! We'll be your friends, honey!" the strapping Dutch gal tried to assure her.

Longarm murmured, "She means she's got no kith and kin left. She and her kid brother were orphans."

"Our father was a redskin and our mother was an outcast ruined woman!" Sally sobbed.

Longarm patted her hand and said, "Aw, mush, he fell for the Union and she died owning land, Miss Sally. I know you don't believe me, but you're going to be all right. You still got property and your honest job at the hotel. Your brother would want you to carry on."

Sally shuddered and said, "I'll never go back to that hotel, never, not even to change my clothes and they can send me any wages they owe me! It was awful, Custis. He'd coughed up blood all over the dusty cement floor and as soon as I see to what they left of the poor boy I want you to take me home. My own home, where our mother died and I have flowers to pick for both their graves!"

Longarm nodded but suggested, "Why don't we carry you home right now to wash up, change your duds and rest up a mite whilst I work things out with them, here?

93

I don't want to upset you, Miss Sally, but there's no way we can plan on a funeral for a day or more."

The nurse from the doc-cum-coroner was shooting warning glances at him. But Longarm said, "The truth may hurt. But we all want to know who shot the boy and there has to be . . . an investigation."

"They're not going to cut him open, are they?" Sally sobbed. As her white blood took command of her broken heart.

Longarm quietly replied, "Just enough to see how many bullets that jasper put in him, and what sort of bullets they were, Miss Sally. Think of it as like when a doctor has to lance a boil or take out some tonsils. Nobody wants to cut kids any more than they have to. But they have to cut where some cutting must be done."

As if to change the subject, the nurse said, "I'll stay with her all the way, but do you think it's safe for us to take her out to their homestead with that . . . mean thing running loose?"

Longarm shrugged and admitted, "Nope. But he just now proved Bobby would have been as safe at home or safer. He had no yard dog down in that basement with him and might have felt too well hidden for his own good."

He rose, adding, "I'll go hire us a rig. The killer could have got at Miss Sally, here, without risking a trip to parts of the premises off limits to the public. After that he has no call to come after her. Bobby saw him kill Luke Warner and knew his face. Miss Sally, here, couldn't testify against him if we asked her to. So he'd be a fool to go to the home address of his last known victim!"

By the time he got back from the livery with a hired one-horse Studebaker Sally had her nerves under better control. The two gals talked in the back as Longarm drove. The nurse just kept agreeing as Sally decided she might drill in some garden truck for later in the year when the herds came through, or mayhaps sell out and use the money to put herself through finishing school, unless she chose to take up landscape painting. It was easy to see she just didn't know what she wanted to do, now that she had no little brother to worry about. Another, somewhat older gal Longarm knew of had gotten middle-aged and fat taking care of an ailing mother, then killed herself after her mother died and they wouldn't let her join that opera company. It was easier to daydream about a someday-when-you-were-free when you had someone or something holding your feet on the ground.

At the neat but modest frame set amid flower beds and a kitchen garden on the last five acres of a once-bigger homestead, with way bigger and newer houses all around, Longarm and the nurse waited in the small front parlor whilst Sally splashed around in the back.

The nurse, who said he could called her Frieda Arnhorst, put her blond head closer to whisper, "I was trying to hush you, but you would go on about that damned autopsy!"

He shrugged and said, "Somebody had to tell her she couldn't bury her kid brother right away, didn't they?"

Frieda said, "No. The undertaker who runs the drugstore works with us a lot. Dr. Templar is the deputy coroner for Hardwater. He was in the back with them as they were embalming the poor boy this afternoon!"

Longarm nodded approvingly and said, "I stand corrected and I thought he seemed to know his business when he tore open Pete Breen's shirt this morning. How is the marshal right now, by the way?"

Frieda said, "He wants to get up and go after the unmentionable act who wounded him and murdered Bobby Arrowmaker and those others. We're keeping our fingers crossed. It's been our experience that a flesh wound heals within six weeks or mortifies within days. We've irrigated and sutured the small hole on his chest and the bigger one on his back. If we see crimson inflamation and yellow puss with no fever within forty-eight hours it ought to be safe to send him home to recover. If we see black flesh, green puss and a sweaty feverish thrashing . . ."

"I was in a war one time." Longarm quietly cut in, adding, "How soon do you reckon they'll release the body to Miss Sally?"

She answered, "Most any time, now, unless they discover he was poisoned with something exotic instead of getting shot. He told his sister he'd been shot, and who did it. He has two bullet holes in his chest. The bullets were still in him when he died at the clinic before Dr. Templar could do much for him. I, for one, will be very surprised if they're not U.S. issue pistol rounds. Probably .45-28. Anything more powerful should have gone through the poor boy, like the one that struck Marshal Breen from across the street."

Longarm nodded thoughtfully and said, "That could add up to two gunslicks, as described at the livery down Kanorado way. The one who gunned down the bartender, brand inspector and other stable boy did so with an underpowered army pistol. It's commencing to look as if he used the same gun on Bobby Arrowmaker. The one shooting at Marshal Breen and me, earlier, did so with S-and-W .44-40 rounds. I found some of his brass atop Steiner's hardware. So the two of them sure must have felt ambitious this morning, and I wonder where their ponies were whilst all this was going on."

The strapping blond suggested, "Wherever they've been hiding out all the time. There's something I've been wondering about U.S. Army Ordinance. I heard Dr. Templar and Marshal Breen talking about it as we were tending to his wounds this morning. Does it make sense to arm our soldiers with underpowered pistols and single-shot rifles at a time when any Indian who saves his allotment money can buy repeating rifles and side arms that hit almost twice as hard as those .45-28 Schofields?"

Longarm said, "The War Department is at war with itself over that, Miss Frieda. With both sides making their own brands of sense. Your average army recruit, these days, is a greenhorn of Irish or Dutch persuasion, no offense, who was never allowed to handle any sort of gun before he got to this land of opportunity. So the army has to train him from scratch and it's hard to teach a green gun hand not to flinch as he pulls the trigger, braced for the kick."

Funny noises were coming from the back now. Hoping a nurse would never suspect a mere man of recognizing the wet hissing of an India rubber douche bag, Longarm continued, "They've been phasing out the breakfront, rapid-loading but underpowered Schofield for Colt's newer model, marketed as the Peacemaker. But the Schofield was popular with cavalry troopers for the same reasons a heap of pistoleers find it a bargain at government-surplus prices. It hardly kicks and reloads quickly, at full gallop if need be, and as we've just seen, throws a man-sized .45 slug hard enough to down its intended target. As for the single-shot Springfield Conversion .45-70, it kicks like a mule and throws the same slug a country mile, with considerable accuracy. So the notion fielded by *that* war department faction was that green troops should be taught to shoot straight without wasting ammunition by blazing half a magazine away at the same Indian. Some of them same Indians were packing repeating rifles at Little Bighorn and I understand they had some heated discussions in Washington before the slow but sure faction won the day."

She shrugged and added, "All the Indian veterans of

97

Little Bighorn are hiding out in Canada or settled snug on their reservations in spite of Mr. Oliver Winchester. So there's something to be said for both ways of shooting."

There came a sort of imperious rapping on the front door. Frieda called out, "I'll get it!" and sprang up to do so, admitting a sort of imperiously handsome woman in summer-weight widow's weeds but no hat atop her pinned-up and gray-streaked hair. Unless her once-darker hair was going gray ahead of time, she sure took good care of herself. The willowy form inside that expensive, black-silk outfit wasn't bad, either.

As Longarm rose to his feet without his own hat the strapping blond introduced her as one Edwina Norwich. The widow Norwich barely brushed across him with her cast-iron eyes to tell Frieda, "I just heard. I've been keeping their hound, Chunky, for the poor boy while he was staying in town. Where is she?"

Frieda said, "In the back, freshening up. She's . . . indisposed at the moment."

The older woman said, "Nonsense, I'm her neighbor!" and tore back through the curtained doorway, trilling, "Sally, dear, where are you? It is I, Edwina!"

"*Vulture* is the term she was searching for!" bitched the nurse as she sat back down next to Longarm.

He said, "You'd know everyone in this town better than I do, ma'am. But ain't it considered neighborly to pay a call on a dead boy's kin and ask what they want you to do about his dog?"

The strapping blond curled her lip to reply, "What'll you bet she was charging poor Bobby room and board? Their yard dog's name isn't Chunky, by the way, it's *Shunka*, meaning dog, in Osage. Even I know that and I look less like an Indian than that spiteful snob!"

98

Longarm mused, "She did seem sort of frosty just now. What was that about her being a vulture?"

The gal who lived in Hardwater explained, "She landed here the first time just as they were laying out the Ogallala Trail along the state line and Hardwater commenced to sprout around a smithy by a water hole. Edwina Norwich had just flown up from the flint hills on her widespread vulture wings, to start buying cheap and selling dear. She got a quitclaim on the deserted Muller homestead for next to nothing and sold it to the township as a herder's campground for a scandalous profit. Most of the new homes you can see from yonder front window stand on proven homestead land Edwina diddled Sally and Bobby out of, since their mother was no longer here to protect them. I understand she was the one who talked both those freeborn Osage kids into taking menial jobs in town, lest they manage to show a profit on land she wanted for herself!"

Longarm shrugged and pointed out, "Working for day wages as a hotel maid or stable hand ain't all that menial, next to trying to scratch a living out of barely enough marginal range to graze two dozen cows. I know you've heard this said before, most every time the herds pass through, but without expensive irrigation you just can't grow a thing more profitsome than cows on natural shortgrass prairie. I was just down to that newer Macropolis homestead and even though they're now raising more pigs and chickens than they have enough water for, that one younger brother has to work in town as a barkeep to make ends meet. As for them kids living all that freeborn, ain't nobody gets to live without working when they ain't born rich. For all the romantic blather about noble savages by writers who seem to have met mighty few savages of any breed, Mister Lo, the Poor Indian, left to his druthers, worked as hard or harder to feed his family. Albeit I'll allow there may be more fun in chasing your supper on the hoof instead of buying it in cans with money you earned at some steady job. But running buffalo is a young man's chore whilst a man can work at a steady job until he's old and gray. After that the kids are breeds who's Indian daddy had a steady job, lest we feel the Majestic Hotel and Municipal Corral have been taking unfair advantage of them."

The strapping blond snapped, "You men are all alike when it comes to dedicated bitches with trim waists and well-turned ankles! I might have known you'd defend her!"

Longarm said, "Ain't defending nobody. Calling the shots as I see 'em and, as for her ankles, I hadn't noticed. But I reckon I'll glance on down, the next chance I get."

Chapter 12

The widow Norwich and Sally Arrowmaker came out together arm in arm, with Sally looking more country in her best Sunday dress than she had in her hotel uniform. Neither one had ugly ankles. Edwina Norwich announced, "It's all settled. Poor Sally and her Chunky will be staying with me until after the funeral. I've directed them to send word as soon as they have Bobby over to the church. Would either of you care to join us for some tea next door?"

Frieda said she had to get back to the clinic. Longarm said he had to get her there. So they parted stiffly polite, with Longarm's smile more sincere.

Driving side by side back to town, Frieda sniffed, "What will you bet she's talked that poor child out of the last of her property by the time we get out of this buggy?"

Longarm said, "I check books out of the Denver Public Library when I run low on pocket jingle closer to payday. So I've read what Mr. Karl Marx has been writing from London Town about buying and selling property. Seems to me there's be no point in owning property if you weren't allowed to sell it, and nobody could sell it if nobody was allowed to buy it."

The strapping blond protested, "Not at such outrageous advantages! They say Edwina's bought run-down town houses for their back taxes, slapped a coat of paint on them, and resold them for hundreds of dollars!"

He shrugged and said, "They call that 'Price and demand,' ma'am. An egg you could buy in Denver two-for-a-penny will cost you a dime up in the goldfields, where they got more gold mines than chickens. Miss Edwina can't be the only one who's gotten in on the ground floor of a mushrooming trail town. A heap of early birds figure to get rich off others by hardheaded business dealings, and as long as they stay within the letter of the law that ain't no business of mine."

She said he didn't understand what it was to be used and abused in a cold, uncaring world.

He said, "I was born on a hard-scrabble hill farm in West-by-God-Virginia and what of it? This cold, uncaring world ain't fixing to let Jay Gould or J. P. Morgan live more than a hundred years longer than your average mayfly or eat much more than the rest of us without getting sick. Things are rough all over and I have enough trouble with the folk who endanger persons or property with deadly weapons, Miss Frieda. Right now you're tending to a shot-up town marshal and we have a dead boy's killer at large as well."

Frieda said, "It's his sister I'm concerned about. Edwina Norwich means to diddle her out of their last holding here in Hardwater!"

Longarm let it go. He could see the big, strapping blond didn't want to hear a breed gal with no kith or kin in a dinky trail town might do better starting over somewhere else with even a modest grub-stake, or how she'd surely be safer holed up with a rich widow and her servants than alone in that frame, come sundown.

He dropped the nurse off at the clinic and returned the

hired rig to the livery before he got his saddlebags and Winchester from their tack room to tote them back to his hotel.

He put his possibles away and wedged another match stem under the door hinge before he went downstairs in his shirtsleeves, vest and six-gun, seeing it was warming up. He found young Tim Colson and yet another kid deputy scouting for sign ahead of him in the basement.

He gained some respect for his juniors and saved himself some time when Tim gave him a grand tour of the fairly well-lit blood-spattered cement betwixt the changing room the spatters led out of to where Bobby Arrowmaker had been found in the furnace room by his sister.

Tim said, "We canvased the staff and other guests. Nobody heard the shots. But the blood's barely dry in some places, and the timing may work if somebody shot him with short rounds down here underground at the same time that other cuss was blazing away from a rooftop with high-powered .44-40 rounds."

Longarm hunkered down, guestimating how long it took blood to dry that much on porous cement. Then he rose to go on back to the room Bobby had been staying in. He could see why she'd waited until she got home to douche, poor little thing. There was only the one rumpled cot, with blood on the bedding as well as all over the bare floor. He remembered, even as he scouted the cement walls in vain for sign, that the bullets had stayed in the unfortunate breed.

Bobby should have brought a gun from home. There didn't seem to be one. The killer had either carried it away or he'd had one hell of an easy chore that morning.

Longarm made the kid deputies feel good by allowing their notions made sense and telling them to keep up the good work.

Then he ambled down to the Western Union to read

103

the wire from Fort Sill as he retraced his steps to the clinic, where he found Marshal Breen feeling left out and raring to go.

Longarm nodded at Frieda, standing in the doorway with her arms folded as if to block it, and told the older lawman, "You can't. If you could we've got all the bases covered. I just got a wire from a pal with the B.I.A. They keep casual tabs on anybody who was ever on their rolls as an allotment-drawing Indian, whether they're still on the B.I.A. blanket or not. Depending on whether times are tough or things off the reservation are booming, folk are always changing their minds whether they feel Indian or white. Had the carpetbaggers ever put through that Forty-Dollars-and-a-Mule proposal for the freed slaves, the B.I.A. and me suspect a heap of rain dancers would have suddenly remembered they were colored. But, be that as it may, the Arrowmakers are still listed at Fort Smith as sometimes Osage. They don't have anything on the other names you gave me for breeds or possible breeds, but, as Alice Macropolis pointed out, I could be wasting time on that angle. The mysterious stranger who convinced an Osage breed he was an Osage full-blood could have hailed from most any Indian nation. For I don't hail from any and I still know what *shunkawakansota* means."

The marshal and his blond nurse exchanged glances. Breen laughed and said, "You do, huh? Why don't you let us in on it, Paleface?"

Longarm smiled modestly and said, "*Shunka* means 'dog,' *wakan* means 'medicine' and *sota* means 'blue-gray,' adding up to a blue-gray medicine dog, or blue roan."

Frieda objected, "I thought those kids once told me *shunka* meant just plain 'dog' in Osage. But don't they say *tashunka* for 'horse'?"

Longarm nodded but said, "They use the prefix for an

important he-critter, so *tashunka* literally means big-tough-he-dog but they use it for a stallion. Horses ain't an Indian invention. They never saw any horses before Comanche stole the first ones off the Spanish, down Texas way. So in all the Indian dialects horses are described in more familiar terms as medicine-dogs, elk-dogs or whatever. They don't have their own names for honeybees, neither—they call them white men's flies—but whilst I'm teaching you all to speak Osage those two white men tracking some blamed sort of Indian are still at large, and still on the prod, from the way they've carried on, so far, today."

Breen said, "I've been thinking about that, lying slug-abed with time to study on this morning. They were just as likely out to kill you, Longarm. I've been here all along and you were right next to me."

Longarm said, "I mean to ask them as soon as I catch up with them. I can see how most any lawman would be a tempting target to a hired gun. Some of their other targets make no sense at all. That federal brand inspector they never should have shot had no possible connection I can see with that other gunslick they seem to be after."

He turned to ask Frieda how soon she thought they'd be able to bury Bobby Arrowmaker.

She said, "Dr. Templar just released the body, in his capacity as deputy coroner. I suppose it will be up to poor Sally whether she wants him to lie in state or get it over with. Why do you ask?"

He said, "I'd best put off my canvasing of outlying spreads until she sets a time. I feel I ought to be there. No way I could cover even the spreads known to have Indians on 'em betwixt now and supper time."

Breen asked, "What if you never find any breeds or full-bloods who can tell us more about that first killer?"

To which Longarm could only reply, "I'll have to find

him some other way. The funny part is, it ain't him they've sent me after. I pack no warrant on him for that killing down by Fort Sill. I'm after the white man who gunned Brand Inspector Chambers and *he's* after that mysterious Indian, ain't that something?"

Breen pointed out, "Neither one of them nor the horses you said they might be riding have been seen in Hardwater all day. My boys have been asking. You did say they were riding a buckskin and a cordovan, didn't you?"

Longarm replied, "The liveryman in Kanorado said they were. I have yet to lay eyes on the rascals or their mounts. So by now any crook with a lick of sense might have changed horses, more than once. Remind your boys they're looking for a hawk-faced cuss wearing a low-slung Schofield .45-Short and most anyone else packing a substantial pistol, rifle or both, chambered for the more popular and higher powered S-and-W .44-40 rounds."

"And what if we never find hide nor hair of either here in Hardwater?" the town law demanded.

Longarm said, "It'll mean they couldn't find the one they came here to kill. I've a fair notion where they might head from here for some further orders and at least some expense money. I'd have already headed down that way if I hadn't feared they'd make a good Indian out of Cracker Marner's killer and be on their merry way. I wish it was tougher to wire money orders most anywhere on the infernal map."

He was explaining about the Widows Marner when Doc Templar joined them, holding a tin tray with two mangled blobs of lead in it out to them as he marveled, "The Arrowmaker boy was tough for his size if he made it that far from the cot he was sitting on. I make these slugs we dug out of him .45-Short, deliberately mangled out of shape before they were fired to chew the victim's insides out, as they just about did!"

"What did they shoot the marshal, here, with?" asked Longarm. Doc Templar said, "I told you earlier, there's no way to be sure when there's no bullet to recover, but no twenty-eight grains of powder would have drilled clean through a grown man at that range. Getting back to Bobby Arrowmaker, I just told that colored boy who works for the widow Norwich they can have his body anytime. Won't need that for the inquest I'll be calling tomorrow morning. There's no mystery about the cause of death. We only need to know who put these bullets in the poor kid!"

Longarm said he'd check back later and Frieda walked him out front, muttering murderously, "Aren't you going to do anything about the way Edwina Norwich has taken poor Sally Arrowmaker captive, Deputy Long?"

Longarm replied, "My friends call me Custis and what that other woman might or might not be doing to comfort Miss Sally or mayhaps take advantage of her just ain't my beeswax. It's a free country. Miss Sally is free, half white and over twenty-one. It's up to her whether she wants to sell her home, turn it into a house of ill repute or drill in more garden truck, as she was threatening to before. I bet you vaccinate kids for the pox whether they want to be vaccinated or not, right?"

She laughed despite herself and said, "God will get you for that. So, all right, we're both inclined to be authoritarian. It comes with our jobs. But it just makes my flesh creep to picture poor young Sally signing on the dotted line as that greedy old bitch weeps crocodile tears over a boy she probably looked down on as a breed!"

Longarm gravely replied, "I find it hard to picture crocodile tears leaking out of a bitch-dog's face, and do you know for a fact the lady you're mean-mouthing ever said a word low-rating either of the Arrowmaker kids?"

The High Dutch blond said, "No, but anyone can see

Edwina thinks she's the bee's knees and poor Sally has nobody to look after her!"

Longarm said, "I suspect Miss Sally can take care of herself more than she might let on, and as for anyone helping her out, everyone from Miss Edwina to Doc Templar inside seems to be smoothing things for her more than, well, present company."

She gasped as if he'd pinched her fair-sized rump and spun to flounce inside, slamming the door after her, hard.

He didn't see anything of her or any of the other ladies until they held that candlelight service for Bobby Arrowmaker that evening and buried him in the churchyard as the full moon rose to smile down at them all, the same as if he'd been a pure Christian *Wasichu*.

Sally had seemed distracted all through the funeral rites. Edwina and Frieda had both been exchanging dirty looks at one another and staring at him more thoughtfully until, at last, they planted the fool kid in the ground and Longarm felt free to slip away to go back to his hotel and shed the boiled shirt and tie he'd put on for the occasion. He was on shank's mare, the churchyard being too near his hotel to justify saddling and then having to unsaddle either of his hired ponies. Like-minded others were walking back to the center of town in the gathering dusk and he paid little mind until the heel clicks keeping pace with him on the right told him Sally was on her way back to the Norwich place in another buggy. A Berlin drawn by a matching pair that evening.

Longarm wearily replied, "I'm just as glad I don't have to worry about her at the hotel. In case them killers are still lurking about, I mean. I'll bet you make lots of friends, managing to make a Berlin sound like something down and dirty instead of a handsome carriage."

She didn't answer for a time. When she did, she confided in a lost child tone, "I want to have friends. I try to be friendly, Custis. But no matter what I say you seem to take it as some sort of nasty remark. Can't you see I want to be . . . friendly?"

"It aint easy." Longarm confided, adding, "I'll try to keep it in mind you're just inclined to send mixed signals, and if we had time to sort them out, I'd be proud to try."

She slipped her arm through his elbow, gasping, "Oh, would you? My place is just up the way and I missed supper, leaving directly from the clinic when my relief showed up this evening. How would you like me to warm up the knockwurst and sauerkraut I'd set aside in my ice-box this morning?"

To which he could honestly reply, "That sure has any other plans I'd made for this evening beat, Miss Frieda."

Chapter 13

She had no old-country ways of talking and she said she'd gone to a nursing school in Ohio, but as soon as you smelled Frieda's kitchen you suspected she was a second-generation midwestern gal.

Knockwurst and sauerkraut took some boiling. So she changed into a housedress less severe than her uniform and they got to talk some before their late supper. By the time they'd sat down to enjoy her High Dutch cooking with Arbuckle-brand coffee Longarm had a better handle on her lonesome longings. She said she'd always wanted more friends than she'd ever managed to make, with the few gals she'd beeen able to get along with in nursing school as unpopular as her for some reason.

Longarm decided, "The other gals in your class had you down as a clique of sarcastic snobs. It's easy to be taken the wrong way and hurt folk you only want to make friends with when you mix snot with sugar."

She protested, "One has to fight fire with fire. What would you have me say when someone puts me down?"

He said, "Make sure they were out to put you down before you try to pay them back in kind. Back at the

Arrowmaker spread this afternoon you lit into Edwina Norwich when, as far as I could see, she wasn't paying either one of us much mind."

Frieda nodded and said, "Then you did notice how cold she is and yet that didn't bother you?"

He asked, "Why should it? She said she was there to comfort another gal who'd just found her brother bleeding in a furnace room! What would you have had Miss Edwina say to us, glad to see you? Let's take off our duds and stage an orgy?"

Frieda blushed and murmured, "Trust a man to come up with that suggestion! But don't you think she could have addressed us more as . . . social equals?"

He asked, "How come? To her we ain't her social equals. She's one of the richest folk in town and likely pays her butler as much as I make, your own salary being your own beeswax. That's the way this world we're stuck with works, Miss Frieda. If it's any comfort, I'm sure Queen Victoria wouldn't address Edwina Norwich as a social equal, or take her on as a lady-in-waiting. I just can't say how the Dowager Empress of China feels about Queen Victoria. But if Queen Victoria's losing sleep over it I feel sorry for her."

Frieda washed down some knockwurst and asked if Longarm felt sorry for her.

He said, "I don't have to. You're feeling sorry enough for yourself on your own. Everybody has something to feel sorry for themselves about. Nobody has ever been born the omnipotent master of all time and space, and when you get right down to daydreaming, nothing less is ever going to do."

She laughed and said, "What would you do first if you were the ominpotent master of all time and space?"

He said, "I reckon I'd go back to before the times they were writing the Good Book and point out some more

111

sensible commandments. Then I'd do something about the bugs. I wouldn't have to swat one fly, being master of time and space. I could just decree that no fly eggs laid from that day forward would ever hatch. Then I reckon I'd do away with wisdom teeth and pimples. But I'm never going to get such powers and I doubt I'll even make president of these United States. So I reckon I'll just worry about catching the killer of poor old Will Chambers and all those others. How Edwina Norwich feels about my social position ain't likely to matter either way unless she's in on it with them."

Frieda laughed incredulously but said, "Oh, if only! Wouldn't that be rich? It would serve her and her snooty friends right if you caught them aiding and abetting those Texas killers!"

Longarm said, "There you go leaping to conclusions again. I know they said that one who shot Gus Henson and Will Chambers in the Boxelder wore a Texas hat. But my home office suspects he's a notorious west-coast rider called Frisco Harrigan. He's said to ride with this shorter cuss called Pud Barker. Taking my own advice to heart, I've been keeping an open mind until I lay eyes on either of them. Leaping to conclusions can be fatal in my line of work. You're only risking unpopularity by shoving your own hurt feelings inside the skulls of other folk. I got to know for certain whether it's time to go for my gun or not."

She suggested they have their dessert on the sofa in her sitting room. As they were moving the coffee and apple pie, the plain old apple pie invented in High Dutch Frankonia, she asked him why he'd accused her of planting her own hurt feeling in the minds of others.

He said, "Because you've been doing it, Miss Frieda. You have a woman grown who's neither afaid of work nor . . . acting friendly as a poor pathetical freindless or-

112

phan out here in country she grew up in whether you find it all that lonesome or not. You have a rich woman looking down on you when in point of fact I doubt she *gave* toad squat about either one of us or not. You must not think they pay you what you're worth. That's likely why you worry about others guessing at how much you make."

"It doesn't bother you that others might not care about you one way or the other?" she demanded.

He asked, "How are we ever going to know, for certain? All we can go by is what others might do or say. It's *possible* for a best friend to be coveting our assets or our wives but how many friends would we have if we accused them of plotting against us? There's a word the head doctors use for shoving your own words down somebody else's throat. But I disremember it. Suffice it to say I've found it best to take folk at face value until they do or say something worth getting suspicious about. When you suspect everybody of everything you wind up sitting in a padded cell, suspecting yourself of being out to *git* you!"

She sighed and said, "I hope you're right about Edwina Norwich. I confess I've always been better at guessing what you *menfolk* have on your minds!"

He smiled sheepishly and said, "Aw, you have the advantages of your profession as well as your gender. Assuming you look in the mirror now and again you naturally know what all of us are thinking when we look at you, Miss Frieda."

She sighed and said, "I know you think I'm a big, fat cow. I've tried and tried to get back down to the way I looked in my teens, but it's just no use and it hurts to know all of you are laughing as you take off my clothes with your eyes!"

Longarm laughed incredulously and assured her, "When you're right, you're right, and I undressed you

113

with my eyes the first time I saw you bending over on Market Street this morning. But when you're wrong, you're wrong, and the last thing I see when I strip you naked with my eyes is a big, fat cow. You're what they call *Junoesque*, Miss Frieda. Them ancient Romans, who admired the goddess Juno, liked a grown woman to have a little meat on her bones and you've surely filled out swell since those teen years there's just no going back to."

He had her blushing like a rose and telling him he was just saying that to spare her feelings. So he shoved the coffee table with their trays clear of the sofa and took her in his arms to feel her up as he kissed her in a way that seemed to confuse her some.

He let her come up for air in case she had something to say and she asked, "Why are you kissing me like that? Does it mean you want to fornicate when you put your tongue in a girl's mouth?"

He left his free hand on her heroic left tit but decided, "Let's just say I'm trying to be friendly. I ain't so sure we ought to go any further!"

She asked, "How come? I know how to take care of myself if that's what you're worried about and nobody has fallen in love with me since I got out here from Ohio."

Longarm kissed her again, in a more brotherly way until she stuck *her* tongue in *his* mouth. He suggested, "It might be best not to let this get that serious, Miss Frieda. I ain't exactly a prince on a white horse for a maiden-pure to give her all to. I'm a natural man passing through on a chestnut and leading a paint. As soon as I finish up here I'll be drifting on. So . . ."

"Now who's shoving his own words down somebody else's throat, with his tongue for a ramrod?" Frieda laughed, tonguing him some before she took his wrist to move his hand lower, purring, "I only want you to fall in love with me, not to propose holy matrimony! I'm not ready to marry up, yet. I mean to wade in the Great Salt Lake, visit that Grand Canyon and bed at least a hundred men before I settle down for life with the one who can satisfy me every time."

So Longarm told her he knew just how she felt and she murmured through his mustache, "Not on this sofa with our clothes in the way. I'd ask you to sweep me up and carry me into the bedroom if I thought you could!"

Longarm figured he could, so he did and as he toted her across her hall into the darker room she indicated Frieda chortled, "Oh, this feels so romantic! How did you ever get so strong, Custis?"

To which he could only reply. "My folk were naturally big boned and they worked me hard until the fates worked me harder, once I was on my own. I told you we called gals like you *Junoesque*, not fat, Miss Frieda."

She still begged him not to light the lamp and to shut the door of her bedroom before he undressed her. So he lowered her to her big four-poster and rose to go shut the door against the faint sitting-room light that had followed them across the hall. When he got back to her he found she'd shucked herself naked for him. So he kissed her all over as he tossed his own duds, boots and gun belt to the four winds and rolled into the welcome mat betwixt her widespread husky thighs to part it with his old organ grinder as she thrust up to meet him with her throbbing ring-dang-doo.

He felt more comfortable about her virginity, or the lack thereof, as the big, strapping blond commenced to bump and grind as if she was out to buck him off. And she might have, had not she been the one holding on to the saddle horn with her internal muscles. But she was and there was a lot to be said for a naturally big-boned gal who did a heap of honest work on her feet every day.

115

The clinic was open seven days a week and Frieda and that smaller ward boy at the other end of that stretcher were the only ambulance service in a small but bustling trail town.

From her moaning and groaning as he was fixing to come in her, Longarm suspected she felt pleasantly surprised by her own feeling down yonder at the moment. It was hard to tell when a woman clamped down on purpose, but he suspected the big, strapping blond might have started out with a love slit suited to her proportions, and no matter what all smart whores told teenaged customers, a tight fit felt way better than a little lost pecker trying to find its way in the dark.

But since Longarm was a fair-sized man in every way and Frieda had learned along the way to take hold of any situation with all she had to work with, she came just ahead of him and came some more as she felt him shoot his seed up into her.

It felt dumb to have a woman thank you for doing that.

She didn't smoke in bed or anywhere else. She said it was bad for one's health but it was all jake with her if he smoked just long enough to get his second wind.

He decided not to that evening. Smoking alone in the dark wasn't as much as the novelty her healthy notions offered. So they cuddled and talked with their heads on one pillow and their moist lips just brushing as she held his limp dick in one hand lest he draw away.

As they got to know each other better Longarm began to understand why Frieda seemed so suspicious of older women. Such a woman, old enough to be ashamed of herself, according to Frieda, had stolen the medical student who'd taught her how to tense her internal muscles so fine when she'd been younger and skinnier. It made his balls tingle a mite to picture this right-nicely built blond built most any other way.

116

He didn't press her for the details. He'd found that three was only company in bed when the other two were women, and even that had been more distracting than you'd expect, the few times he'd managed to talk two gals into it. But, being wound up, Frieda had to tell him how she'd been robbed of her true love by a wicked older woman, who turned out to be that older medical student's wife.

"What are you laughing about?" Frieda asked, jerking his old organ grinder for attention as she insisted, "He'd told me they'd married up too young and he was fixing to ask her for a divorce as soon as he got his diploma. He said he wanted to marry me, but he was afraid it would hurt both our careers if the faculty found out we were seeing one another on the side."

Longarm kissed her, knowing she couldn't see his expression in the dark, and managed to sound more serious as he gravely assured her he'd heard some married men were inclined to say things like that.

She demanded, "Why did he think he had to lie to me? He knew I liked him and his old gray wife was back home in Indiana. So why did he even have to bring her up?"

"Guilty conscience." Longarm said, "You'd be surprised how often suspects blurt things to me I never suspected. How come you know he had a wife back home in Indiana down as old and gray if you never saw her?"

She explained, "Bruce, that was his name, said she was a year older than him and frigid besides. She *might* have had gray hair. When he told me he was going back to her, on Graduation Day, he said he didn't love her but he needed the house she'd inherited to hang out his shingle and get his practice going. He said he meant to leave her as soon as he could afford to. He said I'd been really swell in bed all through his last year as a student."

Longarm kissed her and rolled atop her again as he

assured her he could buy that last part. But even as she parted her thighs to him Frieda said, "Wait, we have to get one thing straight before we get too fond of one another, Custis!"

He asked what that might be.

She said, "I have my reputation here in this small town to think of. I know you think I'm easy and I guess I am as far as you're concerned. But tomorrow, in the cold, gray light of day, I don't want us carrying on all mushy in front of the whole town!"

He rammed it in hard, feeling downright fond of the good old gal as he crossed his heart and hoped to die if he'd ever tell a living soul she put out.

Chapter 14

The next morning young Deputy Colson wanted to tag along and Longarm was glad to let him. Canvasing on horseback could go smoother when you had a locally known rider with you. Longarm saddled up that paint cayuse and Tim Colson was riding a black Morgan with a blaze and white stockings. Both ponies felt prancy on a crisp spring morn with the dew still on the sprouting shortgrass and purple pasqueflowers all around.

The pasqueflower, like the tumbleweed, was an old-world immigrant that now fit in with the native grama and buffalo grass of the high plains the way cowboys had fit in with Indians to form something new and wondrous.

With Tim Colson's help, Longarm called mostly on spreads where both races could be found. They were mostly white men married up or living less formal with breed or full-blood women. Night riders paid no mind to white men pronging women of darker complexion but could sometimes get ugly, even this far north, when a white woman took up with a man of color or even a Quill Indian. Some of the smallholders close to Hardwater were couples of mixed blood, as Longarm had been told. All of them greeted Tim Colson cheerfully and none of them admitted to recalling a possible Osage on a blue roan or two white men, short and tall, riding a buckskin and a cordovan.

And so things went until Longarm had asked everyone in the township a local lawman could think of. As they headed back in, well after noon, having missed their noon dinners but having consumed a whole lot of coffee and cake, Tim Colson declared with conviction, "Somebody has to be lying like a wet, muddy rug!"

"What was your first clue?" asked Longarm wearily.

The kid deputy, who seemed to have promise, said, "Look at her this way. I'll buy that Indian on the blue roan lighting out to ride fast and far after gunning that Texican in the Boxelder. But wouldn't those killers hired to track him down pay one call on one nester of the same complexion as, like us just now, they tried to cut his trail?"

Longarm allowed he'd considered that.

Colson grumbled, "That one with the Schofield gunned down Gus Henson, your brand inspector and poor Bobby Arrowmaker after asking where he might find that shadowy rider on the blue roan."

"Why do you reckon they wanted to gun Marshal Breen?" asked Longarm.

Tim Colson snorted, "Shoot, anybody can see they was aiming for you, not old Pete. They must be afraid you'll track them down before they can track that other killer down. What do you suppose they told all those nesters we just talked to about talking to us?"

"Not to talk to us, most likely," Longarm conceded, adding in a thoughtful tone, "You'd think at least somebody back there would have the nerve, if those hombres came by to question them, earlier."

"They must have sounded persuasive," Tim Colson

suggested, adding, "I was reading in the papers about that Black Hand bunch over in New Orleans and the tall and the short of it, out this way, have swatted four men like flies and winged a lawman by way of example. Folk who ain't real Americans can be shy about talking to the law, even when they ain't in fear for their lives."

Longarm felt no call to argue whether Indians were regular Americans or not. He followed Tim's drift and he'd had his own troubles trying to canvas the produce market in New Orleans about the Black Hand that time he'd been there on another federal case.

Tim Colson asked him where they were headed, seeing they didn't seem headed back to the Municipal Corral and Livery Services. Longarm told him, "I mean to call on Miss Sally Arrowmaker at the Norwich place, seeing she's part Indian, and to see how she's taking burying her kid brother last night. You go on in without me if you like."

Tim Colson allowed he'd rather, adding, "I ain't wearing a necktie or enough bay rum to matter, and Miss Edwina has a way of looking at me like I have a sign on my back advising one and all to kick my poor, dumb ass!"

Longarm felt no call to argue about that, either. So they parted friendly and he rode on alone, feeling sort of sorry for too big a froggy for the tadpoles in these parts.

Longarm had never been born with a silver spoon in his mouth and he only made about the same as the foreman of a fair-sized outfit. But, as he'd told old Frieda the night before, he'd never worried much about what others might own, or what they might think of him as long as they were polite about it. He knew from pillow talk with other rich widows how lonesome a no-longer-young lady could get when nobody but obvious fortune hunters or an occasional cuss who just didn't give a shit about her bank account and fancy ways might come along. He'd once been pleasantly surprised by a famous opera singer who hadn't had any for ages, touring the West with tenors scared shitless of such a prima donna.

But as he rode on to the copper-roofed mansion dominating the other new homes all around it, freshly painted for the summer coming on, he had to ask himself, "Are you thinking with your brain or with your old organ grinder, you horny peace officer? You don't know toad squat about Edwina Norwich and now that's two folk who know her better and consider her bad news."

He rode on, demanding that still, small voice of reason to riddle him a sensible motive for a Hardwater widow woman to avenge the death of a married-up Texas blowhard.

As he rode into the dooryard of the imposing pile, he muttered aloud to his paint, "Had Cracker Marner been her secret lover, he'd have hardly staggered from Fat Edna's house of ill repute to get his fool self shot in that Boxelder Saloon. But I'll ask her if she even laid eyes on the ruffian."

He dismounted to tether the paint to a horse-head hitching post out front. As he mounted the veranda stairs the big front door up ahead opened wide to reveal the lady of the house, herself, smiling down at him in a less widow-some housedress of undyed raw silk the color of autumn leaves.

She said, "Forgive the informality. My butler is driving Sally Arrowmaker down to the railroad in my Berlin. But my kitchen help can rustle us up some tea if you like."

He ticked his hat brim to her at the top of the stairs and said he'd just had all the coffee and cake he'd ever wanted. As she led him inside he explained how he'd ridden all over the township to be served coffee and cake instead of a thing he could use. As they entered her front parlor and sat down by a Boston fern in a lace-curtained bay window he asked who Miss Sally might have gone to meet at the railroad stop in Kanorado.

His older hostess said, "Nobody. She'll be getting on. I gave her a fair price for her property and offered to find a good home for her dead brother's dog. It's out back with my purebred chow chows for the indefinite future. Lord knows I'll never sell that shaggy yellow hound for enough to matter."

He smiled thinly across the gap betwixt them as he replied, "No doubt you'll find someone willing to take any yard dog for free. It ain't my business to ask how much you offered Miss Sally for all she had left to hold her here. But I doubt you'll lose money on *that* deal, no offense."

She said, "None taken. I don't expect anyone to think I'm in the real estate business for my health. Before he died and left me some, my late husband told me one could never go wrong buying land, since they were never going to make any more than there already was. Are you sure you wouldn't care for some tea and scones? Scones are these Scottish pastries one has with real English tea from India."

He said, "I've et Scotch scones, and Russian fish eggs served with French bubble wine, Miss Edwina. You go ahead and have anything you like from your own pantry. But, like I said, I'm full and, to tell the truth, it was Miss Sally I hoped to have a word with this afternoon. Her being part Indian and all."

The white widow woman shrugged and said, "It appears our Sally means to go back on the blanket for a time. She said something about going back to some military outpost where she has some relatives on her father's side. She would go on about her father in that shabby quasi-military uniform. I've always understood Indian scouts were carried on the payroll as extra help, hired by the month."

Longarm nodded and said, "Same as the white scouts, medical staff and other extra hands around a military reservation, ma'am. But the Indians hired alongside white scouts like to *quasi*, like you said, in cast-off army blue and organized in platoons attached to regular troops, lest somebody take them for Mister Lo in the heat of battle. Buffalo Bill and Pawnee Jack might be safe riding point in fringed buckskins, but riding into an army camp at twilight in the same can take fifty years off the life of a scout with Indian features. So the army lets them play soldier, and since Little Bighorn they've tended to listen to their advice a tad closer."

She sniffed dismissively and yanked a nearby bellpull as she said she'd never been able to figure out which Indians could be trusted and which you had to watch out for. She didn't need to tell him she felt safer with a white butler and a colored staff. Longarm had been warned she looked down on other white folk. He felt no call to tell her he'd found folk of all compexions and social standings to be good, bad and mostly in-between. Had he thought it might make a lick of difference he could have told her the natural weaknesses of the bulk of the human race made it easy to truthfully point out drunken Irishmen, cheap Jews, lazy colored folk and fiendish Indians of any nation. To date there had never been one recorded incident betwixt the Havasu along the Lower Colorado and even one Anglo or Mex-American. Yet he knew that if he had real money riding on the bet he'd be able to find at least one hot-tempered, murderous Havasu and, since he was looking for two white killers at the moment, he said, "I ain't after any Indians this afternoon. They are. The ones who killed Miss Sally's kid brother along with three others."

The colored maid came in with a silver salver heaped with the makings of a high tea. She was no fool. High tea was what high-toned English ladies called something less than supper but more than coffee and cake. So aside from the scones, or snooty rolls, there'd come a neat pile of dainty sandwiches with the crusts cut off and some of those Napoleon petty frogs that looked like frosted cakes meant to be served in a dollhouse.

Longarm had said he was full and he'd meant he was full. But he accepted a cup of tea with neither cream nor sugar, Chinese style, as she asked why he'd wanted to talk to that breed child if he wasn't interested in Indians.

He explained, "Bobby Arrowmaker told us the mysterious stranger who rode in and out on a blue roan last summer was an Osage. The state of Colorado wants him for shooting a resident of Texas and Texas would doubtless like to hang him, too. But I ride for the federal courts and that first shooting was no federal offense. The killing of a federal brand inspector was. So I want the white man who shot the late Will Chambers and he, in turn, seems to be after that same Osage on the blue roan. It ain't as complicated a picture as all that when you connect the dots with one pencil line."

She nibbled a scone, dainty as a warehouse rat, and said she got some of the picture. Then she asked, "Who do you think those killers are riding for?"

He answered, simply, "Quite possibly the same spitesome widow woman, if not her daughter-in-law. I suspect the late Cracker Marner recognized a hired gun his momma had hired to gun the Indian who'd once scalped his daddy. It ain't smart to holler across a crowded saloon at a professional assassin on some other job for somebody else. So the Osage who'd avenged his daddy shot Cracker Marner before he could spout off any family secrets and rode on. Then, when they heard down home about his

125

being gunned down for no serious reason by a slim dark stranger wearing a Colt Lightning low and tied down. One or both of the Widows Marner figured out who the killer was and so one or the other, maybe both, hired the two who showed up just after the spring trails got passable to avenge *that* dead Marner as well."

She said, "You're right. You do start to see a pattern as you run a line between the dots you can be more certain about. But wouldn't it be easier to just go down to Texas and bring those two spiteful widows in for questioning?"

He asked, "On what charge? The last I heard, they're both rich and you've likely noticed rich widows don't have to take much guff from anyone without a court order to back it up. So far, I'm only *guessing* the way things happened. Even if I'm guessing right, you have to show just cause to get a court order and I just don't know whether to older widow, the younger widow, or neither widow down yonder hired a crew we only *suspect* of being two known killers from out California way."

As there came the sounds of a distant door chime, he never got to go on about birds in the hands or off in some Texican bush. Edwina rose with a puzzled smile and moved to her bay window to peek out, saying, "It's that Deputy Colson from town. I wonder what he wants."

"Likely me," said Longarm, setting his cup aside to rise as he added he'd told Tim Colson he was headed this way and saying, "I suspect Tim noticed that paint I tied up out front, as well."

So they both went to the door and, sure enough, Tim Colson told Longarm, "Old Stavros Macropolis just rode in, all excited, asking for you."

Longarm asked what for and the town lawman replied, "He never said. Ain't sure he knows. He says his squaw, Miss Alice, sent him to town to fetch you. He says Miss

126

Alice has something to show you and a whole lot to tell you."

So Longarm excused himself, or tried to, as Edwina Norwich demanded, "What's going on at the Macropolis spread? I have a right to know. I sold them the place!"

Longarm spun around to ask, "You did? I heard them Greeks got it cheap off a nester who'd failed to make the place pay?"

She shook her steel-rimmed head to say, "I bought it cheap and sold it to Mr. Macropolis at a fair profit. So what's going on out at that pig farm that I don't know about?"

To which Longarm could only reply, "I don't know. I'll come back and tell you after I find out, Miss Edwina. You weren't planning on going anywheres, were you?"

When she allowed she hadn't, Longarm nodded curtly and said, "I hope you mean that. I can't connect the dots worth spit unless I can get some to hold still!"

Chapter 15

As they rode downwind together Tim told Longarm that Greek Stavros had stayed behind to steady his nerves with his own kid brother's help at the Boxelder Saloon. So they found Alice Macropolis alone out front, pacing the stinky dooryard in her bare feet. Her ankles weren't bad, either. It seemed a shame she'd been stuck with that face. Heaps of Cherokee women were sort-of pretty.

As they dismounted and tethered, the full-blood married up with a Greek repeated what her man had said about her wanting to show something to the law.

They followed her around some pigpens and betwixt two chicken coops to a lean-to stable, open to the front, where two ponies were tied next to a span of mules.

One pony was a buckskin gelding. The other was that dark sable shade called cordovan. Alice Macropolis said, "They told us they'd come back and kill us if we told. But that Bobby Arrowmaker hadn't done anything to those white boys and they had no call to kill him."

"Keep talking, ma'am," Longarm suggested in a politely serious tone.

She said, "They made us swap our own riding stock

for this pair. What will you bet they stole them both?"

"No argument about that, Miss Alice. What are the two of them riding right now and how long a lead might they have on us?"

She said, "They rode in around two hours ago. I confess we were afraid to tell on them at first. They swapped for our matched bay geldings. Both old cavalry mounts with some riding left in them."

Tim Colson asked, "Both branded U.S. on the shoulder, ma'am?"

She nodded and said, "We're going to miss them. Had them both since we rode up from Fort Smith on them last year. I suppose you want to know how they thought to come out here to swap after they shot the marshal and that Arrowmaker boy just yesterday?"

Longarm allowed that might be helpful.

She said, "They were out here earlier. Over a week, the first time. They offered to pay for water and some cracked corn for these ponies. We took the money. We needed it. They came back later when I was alone to offer me more money on the side. I took it. We needed it."

"That's betwixt you and your husband," said Longarm, "Such doings ain't a federal offense."

She looked startled and snapped, "I never screwed either one of them! They paid me to tell them things. They wanted to know how long my brother-in-law, Spyros, had been working at the Boxelder Saloon. When I told them he'd just started there this spring they wanted to know who'd been on duty the night some Texas drover had been shot there. When I told them I had no idea they asked about that Osage on the blue roan. I told them true, the same as I told you, that I'm Cherokee and never laid eyes on the rascal no matter what his nation might be. They wanted me not to tell anybody the'd been by. I'm ashamed to say it, but you know I fibbed for them and at

129

the time I did so with a clear conscience. It ain't as if anybody born along the Trail of Tears owes all that much to the laws we never got to write, you know."

Longarm said, "I read about the Trail of Tears. I wasn't there. I wasn't born yet, no offense."

She shrugged and said, "I was. My mother carried me every step of the way, in wintertime. I can't say I grew up fond of any Osage, either. But if that other rider's Osage or not, I hope those two don't catch him. Maybe that's one reason I decided it was best to tell you they were after him on bay ponies marked with government brands!"

"Which way did they ride?" asked Tim Colson, impatiently.

She said, "Southwest, toward the Ogallala Trail."

The younger lawman asked Longarm, "Don't you want to posse up and ride after them?"

To which Longarm thoughtfully replied, "We'd never cut their sign unless they left the trail close to town in broad day. The sun will be down before they can get that far in any direction. So stick with me and you may learn something."

He thanked Alice Macropolis for coming clean abut those ponies as they untethered their own and mounted up.

On the way back to town Longarm considered telling young Tim the joke about the young bull and the old bull, deciding whether to knock down the fence and mount one of them cows or stroll to the gate and mount all of them. He decided it might be best to teach by example.

When they reined in out front of the Western Union the junior deputy brightened and said, "Hot damn! There's no way they could have made it far as Rusty Springs yet, and if they do manage to get around the boys at Rusty

Springs we'll have others covering Kanorado with railroad timetables in their hands!"

But as they dismounted Colson asked, "What if they ain't headed for the railroad? What if they light out east or west across open range?"

Longarm said, "Study on that," as he led the way inside.

Colson did and as Longarm was still composing the first all-points at the Western Union counter the kid decided, "If they leave the well-traveled trails, at this time of the greenup, them big army bays will surely leave dotted lines to cut along! They have to stick to the beaten paths or catch a train clean out of this country and there ain't no railroad stops closer than Kanorado."

As Longarm was composing his second all-points Colson frowned and demanded, "But what if they know we know that? What if they decide to chance a longer run up to the U.P. line at Ogallala?"

Longarm said, "I mean to wire Ogallala and all the smaller towns betwixt hither and you. I'm putting out an all-points on a tall one packing a Schofield and a short one armed with a Colt or Remington .44-40, both wearing Texas hats and riding army bays. If nobody north, south, east or west cuts them off they're better at the game than most. If they're better at the game than most, how come they've been acting so mad-dog reckless up to now? You can't have it both ways. Sly fox and mad dog are a contradiction in terms. I'm warning one and all out ahead of them that they're not only armed and dangerous but crazy as hell or downright stupid-ugly."

As he went on writing Tim Colson said, "Well, I don't know about that. They've surely managed to stay one step ahead of the law as they were getting away with four murders and a damned good try at you or Marshal Breen."

"To what end?" Longarm demanded, handing the all-points over to be sent in every direction as he pointed out to Colson, "If they were hired to track down and take revenge on the killer of that other wild man in a Texas hat, they've surely been going about it mad-dog mean! At least two of the poor souls they gunned down might have been able to help them figure out where that other cuss rode aboard that blue roan. The other two had no connection with the earlier killing as far as I can see!"

As he signed the chit for the telegrams, Longarm added wearily, "I was talking before about connecting dots to form a picture. I've either connected some of the dots wrong or I have too many dots in my damned old puzzle. For connect them as I may, they just don't form any picture at all."

Colson said, "Oh, I know the sort of puzzle you mean. I've seen 'em in the Sunday papers. You run a pencil line from one dot to the other until you wind up with a dog, a cat or a jackrabbit, right?"

Longarm said, "I got too many feet to stand this jackrabbit on. Let's go tell Marshal Breen the little we know and see how he's coming along."

As they rode up to the clinic Tim Colson decided, "I think I see a way to make it work. Let's say that jasper who gunned that Cracker Marner down last summer got away clean. Rode far and wide to parts unknown."

"Then what was he here in Hardwater for?" asked Longarm, adding, "It must have been something worth hanging around for. Had he been free to ride off and never come back, he'd have had no call to gun anybody in these parts. He could have just howdied Cracker Marner, excused hisself to take a leak and vanished forever."

Colson insisted, "Let's say he did. Let's say he gunned down a man who'd surprised him by recognizing him, rid far enough to study on his next best move, and saw his best move was to just keep riding. So let's say it took some time for Marner's kin to get in touch with those other guns for hire, and then give them time to get here six or eight months later with nobody here to use their hired guns on."

Longarm frowned thoughtfully and decided, "I follow your drift. Spiteful widows who hire guns expect to hear some noise unless they get their money back. We used to have acting corporals like that in a war they gave one time. Not knowing what else to do, they ran around camp ordering everybody to salute all rocks and paint all second lieutenants white. But even if that accounts for some needless gunplay I still have too many dots to connect. Cracker Marner's mother could have hired them two, assuming that's who we're after. Or the younger wife of the blowhard trailboss could have hired them to avenge her true love, not knowing how he carried on at Fat Edna's just before he called the wrong man a bastard in the Boxelder that evening. So the hell of it is, I can't charge *both* of them, and if I charge the wrong one first, the other could be long gone or, worse yet, waving a restraining order from her own judge by the time I saw I was barking up the wrong tree. That's what I meant about too many feet on the rabbit or too many roots on the mullberry bush, because I just don't know how the picture's going to turn out!"

They tethered their mounts and went in to see how Marshal Breen was feeling. He said he was feeling poorly. Frieda Arnhorst said he was running a temperature but it was too early to tell how bad his wounds might be mortified.

Old Pete Breen cheered some when they told him about those army bays and the wires Longarm had sent every which way. Breen told young Colson to line up some posse riders for the next morning, ready to ride down the cattle trail to scout for signs of riders leaving the same across open range, unless they got word overnight that they might not have to. Old Breen has seen without Longarm's help how a pair of night riders headed either way along the state line right of way would have to stick to it or leave an easy trail to follow.

Once they'd brought him up to date the older local lawman agreed with Longarm on what happened next. For as he elaborated whilst Frieda listened from the doorway, pretending not to feel excited, there were only three ways it could go. Other lawmen could head the killers off and hold them for Longarm, after which he'd likely get Pud Barker to turn state's evidence, or the killers would get away, in which case Longarm would just have to move in on both the Widows Marner and hope he started with the guilty one, or, all else failing, the killers would get away, both widows would turn out to be innocent and Longarm would be left holding the bag and feeling foolish. That was just the way some cases went. None of them knew where Frank and Jesse were at the moment, either.

Not looking at Frieda, but meaning it for her delicate ears, Longarm announced, "No matter how things turn out, I'll likely have to ride out, come morning. Should anything I uncover lead this way I'll likely be back. If they don't, I won't. So I reckon I'll just get my hired paint watered, foddered and resting up for the trail. Then I reckon anyone who wants to get in touch with me can leave a message at my hotel. The room clerk will be proud to see I get it when I come in."

"Where are you headed after you put your pony away, in case I want to save perfumed paper?" asked Marshal Breen, dryly.

Longarm said he meant to have a word with Spyros Macropolis at the saloon before he got off for the evening. Then he meant to grab a bite to eat and head over to his hotel to see if there were any telegrams or other messages.

He explained, "I asked them at Western Union if they'd leave anything coming in for me at my hotel. Saves my running back and forth when I send wires all over creation. So why don't you try to sleep off that fever and I'll get back to you before I ride out, if I ride out."

Marshal Breen shrugged and muttered, "If I make it through the night," and Frieda moved in to wipe his fevered brow with a damp cloth.

So Longarm said he'd be seeing the both of them, Lord willing and the creeks didn't rise, and left, with Tim Colson tagging after to lead his own pony back to the Municipal Corral.

By the time they'd seen to the comforts of their ponies it was getting on and Tim said he had to go tell his woman to start them an early supper, just in case.

Longarm went to the Boxelder Saloon where he found both Brothers Macropolis at one end of the bar, engaged in a heated conversation in a lingo that was literally Greek to Longarm.

They stopped when they spied Longarm moving in to join them. The older Stavros asked if he and his wife were in trouble, adding that his kid brother, Spyros, had never laid eyes on those saddle tramps.

Longarm said, "I just assured Miss Alice that as long as all she's told us about them pans out true, none of you have busted any federal laws on purpose. You're going to have to return those two livery mounts to their owner in Kanorado. So you figure to be out the price of your sold-off army stock and I reckon that will be punishment enough for being scared of those two scary gents."

Stavros looked relieved and confided, "We got them for ten dollars a head down at Fort Smith. They're not bad horses, for just riding along. But those hired guns will wish they hadn't taken either from us if they ever have any serious galloping to do."

Longarm chuckled and allowed he'd noticed the re-mount service was inclined to hang on to stock with any wind left in it. Then he asked a few questions that jibed with all Alice Macropolis had told him, went back to his hotel and had an early supper of his own, killing time until something worth reading wound up in his pigeonhole in back of the lobby desk.

He ate two desserts and nursed four cups of coffee and half a dozen cheroots before he determined that nobody had headed those hired guns off and that nobody had invited him for a more romantic reading than reading in bed, upstairs.

So old Frieda was either too worried about her rep or too fickle to favor him with another night in her four-poster. That was the trouble with puzzles. You could draw from dot to dot more than one way.

Chapter 16

By sunup Marshal Breen's fever had broken and his wounds were scarlet rimmed with no swelling. So he was feeling better when Longarm dropped by after breakfast.

Frieda Arnhorst seemed to be avoiding his eye as she bustled about other business at the clinic. Longarm had more important things to worry about than the vagueries of the shemale mind.

He told Marshal Breen, "Answers to a raft of wires I sent out have been coming in. It's a pretty safe bet that we're looking for Frisco Harrigan and Pud Barker. They lit out of the California Mother Lode country a bare three weeks ago after a client they'd killed a business rival for up and bragged about it in his cups. He'd only paid them some front money and they can whistle Dixie for the rest, seeing said client sobered up in the Calaveras County jail."

The bedridden older lawman whistled thoughtfully and decided, "That means them spiteful Texas widows could have hired them at modest rates and it would account for some anxious moves. You got to show some results before a client wires you more expense money."

Longarm said, "Nobody's wired any money to anybody from Texas for the past six weeks. I didn't have the pull to get that out of Western Union but my boss, Marshal Vail, does. Hardly anyone from Texas has call to be up this way at this time of the year. If they'd been getting paid by installments the funds have been moving as paper money, sent by mail. Billy Vail's still working on that with the postmaster general. There's a heap of places an envelope might be postmarked."

Breen brightened and said, "Mebbe so, but we only have one postmaster here in Hardwater and he's a pal of Doc Templar. Runs the only drugstore as well. All the mail aimed at anyone in Hardwater Township is sorted by his daughter, Nell. You'd find her back there this very minute unless she's filling prescriptions or sweeping the floor."

Longarm conceded it was worth a try, adding, "If they've been getting money some other way, or not at all, all bets are off. I'm more interested in where they've been hiding out betwixt their sudden flurries of stupid slaughter."

Marshal Breen said, "Oh, Lord, that's right. If they're holed up with somebody we don't suspect, their mail could be sent to them by way of a local name and address. But that still gives Nell a Texas postmark, right?"

Longarm replied, "I said it was worth a try. Meanwhile neither Rusty Springs nor anyone else within a night's ride has reported one bay hair of them two army mounts Alice Macropolis described. Frisco and Pud should have made it that far by now, sticking to the well-traveled roads. So I'm riding with Tim Colson and his posse to see what we can see by circling some."

Then he left without trying to catch old Frieda's eye, whether she was suffering second thoughts, was out to keep him guessing or wanted him to beg.

He rode the hired chestnut barb that morning. The seventeen-man posse rode everything but mismatched stockings or Prince Charming white. Few riders given the choice would ride a pony with both light and dark hooves, albeit either all light or all dark seemed to hold its horseshoes as well. Prince Charming, George Washington and Miss Joan of Arc had been painted on snow white horses. But it was tough to get a cowboy to ride one and Indians thought they were bad medicine. Longarm had never ridden enough white horses to be certain, but he knew a lot of albino cats were deaf or touched some other way.

Tim Colson asked Longarm to lead. So they loped and rested their mounts faster than usual and commenced to circle for sign just a few trailbreaks north of Rusty Springs. It took them past sundown to make the big circuit clean around Hardwater with change and then back up the Ogallala Trail. After they'd seen to their mounts Longarm reported back to Marshal Breen at the clinic before he broke for supper, saying, "*Por nada*. They never left the trail this side of Rusty Springs and nobody in Rusty Springs spied them passing through."

"Then they must have rid north toward Nebraska," Breen opined.

Longarm wearily replied, "I just said that. We did circle a good ways north of here. So if they rode north instead of south they beelined for the Union Pacific line. I wired the Pinkerton railroad dicks, asking them to cover that mouse hole, earlier."

"So now we get to just sit and wait," said the older lawman, not knowing Longarm all that well.

Longarm said, "You do what you like. I'm off for Texas in the morning. Right now I never want to see a saddle again. But I have to return two ponies and catch me a train in Kanorado. Might stop off in Rusty Springs along the way to see a friend of mine."

Breen said, "I thought you told me questioning them Marner widows was a long shot."

Longarm shrugged and said, "If I don't get more encouraging word about those hired guns by sunup that may be the only shot I have left. I have to go talk to that gal at your drugstore post office now."

Frieda Arnhorst never followed him out to the street, even though he walked sort of slow. So, hungry as a bitch wolf, he strode on to the nearby drug-store-cum-post-office-cum-undertaking-establishment.

Nell Bordon, who allowed she assisted her dad in every chore from autopsies to sorting mail, was a vapidly pretty teenager with ash blond hair and big blue eyes set a tad too close together. She told him without having to look it up that nobody in or about Hardwater had received any mail from Texas since Christmastime. Longarm wrote down the names of the two families who'd received Christmas cards from the wrong parts of a big state, even though he couldn't see how that could mean anything to a brace of hired guns who'd have been out California way for Christmas.

As if wanting to be helpful, she asked if he'd like to see all the bullets the deputy coroner and her dad had dug out of everyone so far. Her dad had them in one jar down in the celler.

He declined, saying he'd seen some of them and could guess at the others adding up to .38, .44 or .45 caliber. It had been generally agreed the shadowy cuss who gunned down Cracker Marner did so with a .38 Colt Lightning. "The one firing at Marshal Breen and me from atop Steiner's hardware left .44-40 brass and the four victims of Frisco Harrigan were shot with a Schofield .45."

She confessed, "I've been wondering about that. Just

what do those numbers mean? I can see a .38 caliber bullet is smaller than a .44 or .45. But those two calibers look the same to me."

He explained, "That's because there ain't much difference until you measure them with calipers. Under Anglo-American usage, bullets are measured by hundredths of an inch. If they made a .100 caliber round it would be an inch in diameter. The Brown Bess English musket used by both sides in the Revolution fired a swamping three-quarter inch or .75 caliber ball. During the war they gave in my honor most of the minny balls I ducked were a little over half an inch in diameter, or calibers .51 up to .53 until you got up to the cannonballs. A pistol kicks hard enough firing .44 or .45, five or six hundredths of an inch skinnier than your average minny ball, see?"

She said, "I think so. But while we're on the subject, I noticed that those bullets we took from young Bobby Arrowmaker were all mangled and jagged, as if someone had hammered or filed them."

Longarm said, "Frisco Harrigan is not a nice man. The British troops in India learned that notion from mean Hindus at a place called Dum Dum."

She said, "The bullets we took out of Gus Henson, Will Chambers and Luke Warner, earlier, weren't nearly as distorted."

Longarm shrugged and said, "He may have been in more of a hurry when he gunned the barkeep, a brand inspector and a stable hand in one fit of pique. I reckon he took to whittling some as he brooded about Bobby Arrowmaker being able to identify him as the killer of Luke Warner."

She was either flirting or she had the makings of a good tracker. She asked, "Why do you think he singled poor Bobby out if that was his motive? He shot those other two men in a saloon filled with eyewitnesses. Yet none of them have been shot."

Longarm said, "You mean, so far. Along with motive you have to toss in means and opportunity. Frisco knew where he could catch up with that one witness alone. But now that you've mentioned it, I'll keep it in mind that he might have had some other reason to murder that young breed."

They shook on it and parted friendly. Another lonesome night was coming on, but a man who messed with a gal that young, still living at home, was a man looking for more trouble than Helen of Troy had been worth, as soon as you studied on her.

He dined on steak, potatoes and two helpings of chocolate cake and made it through the night with the help of the *Police Gazette* and *The True Adventures Of Deadwood Dick*, published in London Town. He'd always had a soft spot for farce.

The next day, Frisco and Pud having ridden off to Fairyland on flying horses, as far as anyone could tell, Longarm saddled up and rode out to do things the hard way, stopping over in Rusty Springs after some tedious riding to ride Red Robin right before riding on down to Kanorado, where he returned the barb and cayuse for his deposit and caught the short line out to the east, transfering to a southbound line, then wasting lots of soda pop and dinner in the diner on a sweet little thing who got off at Dodge right after the dessert without kissing him good-bye.

Things happened that way aboard moving trains. But at least he avoided that friendly game of cards in the smoking car and got off an easy buggy ride to the Comanche reserve just outside of Fort Sill in the Indian Territory.

He'd worked with Corporal Kicking Calf of the Indian

police before. So he got invited for noon dinner and served regular store-bought corned beef and Boston beans with flour in his coffee whether he wanted it or not. Corporal Kicking Calf had warned his fellow peace officer not to argue with his bodacious wife. The Comanche friendly was built like many of his nation and one could see why the Comanche had been so anxious to raid the Spanish for medicine dogs. Kicking Calf was of average height with a head and torso that belonged on a seven- or eight-foot giant. He sort of resembled a mighty tall dwarf as he sat there in his blue uniform, going over the assassination of War Chief Eyes-All-Over during the Grant administration.

Kicking Calf recalled the killing with a nervouse smile. Like a lot of Indians, Comanche were uneasy about mentioning the dead, and after that the killer had been sort of spooky, too.

When Longarm described the rider Bobby Arrowmaker had taken for a short, slim Osage, Kicking Calf shook his massive head and sounded certain as he said, "No Osage. No Comanche Eyes-All-Over didn't know as a friend ever got that close to him after sundown, surrounded as he was by his own band. They did not call him Eyes-All-Over because he was easy to sneak up on and his wives said he'd known some crazy *Taibo* woman was after him."

Longarm asked Kicking Calf what else they knew about the crazy white bitch at fcud with the late Eyes-All-Over.

Kicking Calf said, "You people have never understood the rules of War For Fun and Profit. We'd have won if we'd been able to get you to fight our way. Eyes-All-Over counted coup on a *Taibo* settled near the Brazos, many years ago. Many. So he had forgotten about that fight until the dream catchers told him *Hihkiapipuha* had been seen by a servant passing for Mexican, breaking bread with the widow who had been badgering the B.I.A. about her dead husband for years."

Longarm sipped flour-laced coffee long enough to decide how the outlandish Comanche name might translate. Then he asked the Indian police corporal, "Tell me about this Shadow Medicine. An Osage breed I talked to said he seemed to speak Osage."

Kicking Calf shrugged his massive shoulders and said, "I don't doubt it. They say . . . Shadow Medicine is a shape-shifter who can look like a coyote or raven. When you see him up close, this is not easy, he is said to . . . flicker like the shadows back from the firelight. He has been described as young and agile, old and feeble, but always very quiet. We know he speaks Comanche, English and Spanish. So why not Osage or even Apache, which no real people have ever been able to figure out?"

"How did that Comanche servant at the Marner spread recognize such a shape-changing spook?" asked Longarm.

Kicking Calf said, "The crazy *Taibo* woman *called* him Shadow Medicine, in English, in front of a serving *chica* she took for a Mexican it was safe to talk in front of. The Comanche girl pretended not to understand as the two of them plotted the murder of Eyes-All-Over and agreed on the price. The spiteful widow, who did not understand the way things had been in our Shining Times, told Shadow Medicine she would pay a thousand dollars in advance and another five thousand dollars after Eyes-All-Over was dead. The serving *chica* got word to her own uncle, a dream catcher, and he, in turn, warned Eyes-All-Over."

Longarm whistled softly and allowed, "Then this Shadow Medicine must be mighty good as well as moderately rich. There's more to the story than a retired war chief opening the door at dusk to a stranger and paying for his trusting nature the hard way. The old Comanche killer, no offense, was on the prod and surrounded by kith and kin when this other Comanche killer, coyote, raven or whatever appeared out of nowhere to somehow tempt Eyes-All-Over outside where he could be gunned down private. Then Shadow Medicine somehow managed to fade away in the gathering dusk as the whole camp must have looked like a stomped-on ant pile!"

"Shadow Medicine has done that often," Kicking Calf observed, adding, "It is said that once Shadow Medicine comes after one, there is no hope of escaping him or stopping him. How can anyone fight a man who has the medicine to turn into a shadow?"

Longarm shrugged and said, "One might just have to try as best he can. It's a funny thing, but up until now I was feeling sort of sorry for that mysterious full-blood up Hardwater way. I figured he was hiding out from two other hired guns. Now I know he couldn't have been all that worried about them, and tell me something, don't you reckon the murder of a ward of the government on any federal Indian reserve would constitute a federal crime if one wanted to make something of it?"

Kicking Calf said, "If the B.I.A. wants to issue a warrant. Why do you want to go after Shadow Medicine as well?"

To which Longarm could only reply, "Somebody really ought to and it may as well be me."

Chapter 17

The war and recently ended Reconstruction had played
hob with railroad construction in Texas and there was a
lot of Texas to get across, so Longarm had spent three
days in that saddle by the time he got in to Swenson on
the Brazos, riding another livery paint and leading a bigger dapple gray. He left the tired ponies to be cared for
and treated himself to chili con carne over steak before
he went back to the Swenson Livery and asked what they
had for him to ride out to the Marner spread.

They told him the only fresh mount they could hire out
to him was a snow-white charger they'd bought from an
army officer headed back East. Longarm knew they'd gotten it cheap whether it was worth riding through town in
a parade or not. But the day wasn't getting any younger
and he had some miles to travel. So he let them saddle
Old Glacier with his McClellan and they seemed to get
along fairly well until, a mile outside of town, a big prairie
grasshopper buzzed off on its black and yellow wings and
Old Glacier felt it was time for an avalanche.

Longarm stayed aboard—it wasn't easy—and after
crow hopping a spell off the wagon trace through high

chaparral and low branching boxelders the loco albino settled down and didn't spook again until a burrowing owl screeched at sundown.

This time Longarm knew his mount was loco and the ride was less eventful. Longarm had enough sense to dismount and *lead* Old Glacier across the cattle guard in the gap of the barbed wire fronting on the trace along the property line of the combined Marner holdings, a good-sized homespread before you factored in open range and water rights, according to an answering wire Longarm had received.

One of the few things to be said for his long tedious trip down from Hardwater was that, so far, nobody, anywhere, had reported spying hide nor hair of those two known gunslicks riding army bays with War Department brands. Longarm had asked Billy Vail to pull a few strings and intercept any telegrams or interstate mail going in or out of the big spread he'd reached at last. So as he led his white charger along the cottonwood-shaded path toward the rambling, tile-roofed complex in the middle distance Longarm felt fairly certain neither Frisco Harrigan nor Pud Barker could be laying for him up ahead.

Someone who was, in the shadows of the front veranda of the main house, called out through the uncertain light of the gloaming, "Who are you, what do you want and how come you're walking that wedding cake, mister?"

Longarm called back to the unseen male, "I'd be Deputy U.S. Marshal Custis Long. I'm here on government business and I'm walking this poor excuse for a pony because I hate to have folk laugh at me and I've been braced for the dulcet sounds of your yard dogs."

The man in the veranda laughed and called back, "Come on in. We've been expecting you. I'd be the yard dog. They call me Tiny Fulton and I'd be the *segundo* here at the M-Slash-G."

He said something in Spanish, softer, and a muchacho tore out of the shadows to take charge of Old Glacier as Longarm dismounted. Up close where some lamplight spilled out of a front window, Tiny Fulton turned out to be taller than Longarm and built twice as wide across. As they shook, Longarm said he'd just come down from Hardwater and asked whether Tiny had been with Cracker Marner on that fatal trail drive the summer before.

The big foreman said, "That's how I got to be the *segundo* here. Have you lawmen caught that dark, shadowy sidewinder who gunned poor Cracker down?"

Longarm said, "Not yet. How come you've been expecting me? Has somebody wired or written I was headed this way?"

The trap didn't snap. Fulton shook his big head and easily explained, "Read in the papers about that recent shoot-out up yonder. Papers said that cuss with the Schofield was asking about the earlier killing of our Cracker. Doña Ysabela said you or somebody like you would come calling, wanting to know more about Cracker getting shot down like a dog."

Longarm asked, "Which one of the Widows Marner might this Doña Ysabela be? According to my notes, the dead man's mother would be a Miss Melony and his wife would be Miss Dulcenia or, have it your way, *Doña* Dulcenia."

The foreman laughed and said, "Doña Ysabela ain't neither. She's the housekeeper. Runs things for the widow women the way a topkick runs the post for the captain and his adjutant. She gave orders to have you brought to her the moment you arrived and you've been here more than a moment already. I sent another muchacho in to tell her as soon as we spotted you leading that wedding cake in from the wagon trace. So we'd best not keep her waiting. Doña Ysabela has a lot of Aztec mixed in with her high-toned Spanish blood."

As the Texican led him inside and back through the severely high-toned interior, with Oriental rugs atop waxed terra-cotta floor tiles and heavily carved and leather-cushioned chairs and settees against cream stucco walls under gilt-framed oil paintings, Longarm asked where the gals Doña Ysabela ran things for might be.

The *segundo* said, "That ain't for me to say. Doña Ysabela will tell you if she wants you to know."

The mysterious *ama de llaves* as the Mex help likely called her, turned out to be a sort of grotesquely pretty woman of, say, five-foot-two with a head too big for the rest of her. Longarm could see why Tiny Fulton suspected a dab of Aztec along with white blood in her oversized but pretty high-cheeked face. Her big brown eyes were warm and friendly enough as she rose from a sofa near a baronial fireplace in her ivory lace mantilla and low-cut summer frock of peach silk to make him welcome in English and extend her wrist to be kissed, old Spanish style.

Longarm managed to do that without laughing. He'd once bodyguarded the Divine Sarah Bernhardt on a tour of the West. As they sat down together he felt obliged to set his hat aside. He saw there was a dinky cowchip fire going on the grate against the coming chill of a Panhandle evening that early in the year and that Tiny Fulton was nowhere to be seen.

He'd wanted to ask the *segundo* some details about the shooting of Cracker Marner. But old Tiny had been wearing an open-neck shirt and chinked chaps. So he likely knew the parlor of the main house wasn't his place to loiter and gossip.

Doña Ysabela told him he'd be having supper with her at nine, as Spanish-speaking folk were inclined to, staying up way later than Anglo folk, like the North African

149

Moors they'd learned so many other habits from. He didn't want to insult anybody and he'd had that earlier supper before six. So he figured he could manage to eat enough to be polite. Hispanic suppers were protracted as well as late.

It wouldn't have been polite to observe she sure acted as if she owned the whole shebang. But once they'd established who he was and that he'd come to ask quesions about the late Courtney a.k.a. Cracker Marner he delicately raised the question of where in thunder either Widow Marner might be at the moment.

Their imperious housekeeper said the older widow, Miss Melony, was up to the county hospital, feeling poorly. When he asked what might be wrong with the dead man's mother the housekeeper said she didn't know, not being a doctor. She added, "We fear she might have had a, how you say, a stroke? We found her on the floor of her bedroom a short time after we had news of her only son's death at the hands of a man she had once trusted. She could not understand this. She took it very hard."

Longarm nodded soberly and asked in a desperately casual tone, "Did you ever know that rider they call Shadow Medicine, ma'am?"

She looked away, eyelids aflutter, to ask, "Why should you think that?"

He said, "Depends on how long you've been working here. We're not talking about the First Crusade. We know an assimilated Comanche called Shadow Medicine was seen here not too long after the less assimilated Comanche started coming in to Fort Sill around the time Custer was having less luck with the Lakota, farther north. Would it save us some time if I said I knew for a fact that Miss Melony hired Shadow Medicine to run an errand for her up to the Fort Sill reservation?"

She didn't answer.

He said, "You'd have been working here then. Ain't no way they'd have hired an *ama de llaves* out of nowheres. You worked here in a lesser capacity long enough for the Widows Marner to trust you with the silverware and keys to the wine celler. How did you get along with her only son and her Tex-Mex daughter-in-law?"

She didn't answer. She didn't have to. He nodded and said, "I've heard he was a hard-drinking bully, whilst she's said to be a stuck-up *sangre azul*. Is she in the county hospital, too?"

Doña Ysabela made a wry face and said, "I am not at liberty to say where she may be spending the night. You can ask her when she comes back in the morning, if she comes back in the morning. Sometimes she stays . . . away longer."

A colored maid came in to declare supper was about to be served. Longarm was surprised how late it had gotten until he reflected the Texas Panhandle was as far north as North Carolina, where the summer sun set way later than in Old Mexico or even San Antone.

It still felt early for a Tex-Mex sit-down supper. But then as they started with black-eyed-pea soup and the first course of pork chops, grits, white-flour gravy and deep-fried collard greens, he could see why she'd had to reveal she spoke down-home English to get promoted by the elder Widow Marner, née Jukes.

As they ate he told her about those other hired guns somebody she might know had hired to track down Shadow Medicine for killing the man of that house. She repeated that he'd have to take that up with Cracker Marner's widow as soon as she came back. She assured him they'd see to his comforts overnight in one of the many guest rooms but changed the subject every time he tried to ask whether she had a thing to tell him about Frisco Harrigan or Pud Barker.

When he insisted she flared across the table at him, "Stop it! I am not supposed to discuss family matters but I know nothing, nothing about anybody called Frisco or, for heaven's sake, Pud!"

Longarm said, "I doubt either was ever down this way. They left California earlier this year. But somebody got in touch with them for another spiteful job and, well, both the Widows Marner must know you speak English by this late in the game."

She rose from her chair, saying something about not feeling well and getting the servants to show him to his room whenever he wanted. Then she flounced out of the dining room before he could answer.

Longarm told the colored serving maid he could use more coffee but wasn't up to any dessert. He nursed two cups and a cheroot before he got tired of sitting alone there and told the maid the next time she came in he'd as soon turn in now.

She led him through dimly lit corridors to a stucco-walled chamber with jalousies opening on to a patio where flags and lilies marched around a fishpond. The bedstead was a Spanish-style four-poster made in Mexico and draped with mosquito netting. The maid left him the big beeswax candle and said to yank on the pull cord by the head of the bed if he needed anything.

He thanked her and as soon as he was alone he hung up his hat, coat and gun belt, tucked his derringer betwixt the mattress and the headboard and sat down to shuck his boots.

There came a rap on the door. It opened before he could say yes or no. Doña Ysabela came in missing her mantilla, her long black hair unbound, to sort of sob, "That was so

152

stupid of me. Naturally you'd have asked Ellie Mae as soon as I left you alone with her!"

Longarm gravely replied, "Didn't know that was her name. Never asked her anything indecent. This high-toned lady I know down by Galveston observed one time that a man who'd mess with your hired help would doubtless help himself to your silver and spit in your goldfish bowl."

The housekeeper laughed despite herself and said, "That's not what I mean and you know it. What did Ellie Mae tell you . . . about me?"

Longarm said, "Nothing. She never had to. They never said a colored serving maid overheard Miss Melony plotting the murder of Chief Eyes-All-Over, back around '76. They told me a Comanche gal passing as Tex-Mex and pretending not to speak English overheard the interesting supper conversation and got word to her uncle, a Comanche dream catcher. Tiny Fulton and all the help I've seen here so far seem to be Anglo or colored, present company aside. It's all a matter of connecting dots. I never claimed to have any *puha* like your uncle or that other Comanche you warned him about."

She stared thunderghasted, then she decided with a radiant smile, "*En tzare piataibo a tzatipihi*! The real people call you this because you have never been like so many of your people! You have always tried to understand us! And you *do* have medicine! Strong medicine! Hear me, to this day neither of the Marner widows knows I am not a Mexican, and La Doña Dulcenia is Land Grant Spanish!"

Longarm smiled modestly and said, "They pay me to be suspicious and pay attention. After that you'd be surprised how many folk are driven by uneasy feelings to tell me things I never asked. If it's any comfort to you, Miss Ysabela, I can't see how you could be in trouble for warning your uncle that Eyes-All-Over was about to be assassinated. So why don't we just get some sleep and let me worry about questioning the Widows Marner in the morning?"

She said that was jake with her and shut the hall door. As she threw the bolt and came over to blow out the candle Longarm almost asked her what in thunder she was up to.

But he knew what she was likely up to. She was likely out to compromise the arresting officer. It sure beat all how many civilians, male and shemale, thought you couldn't arrest a gal once you'd had your old organ grinder in her.

But, what the hell, he wasn't likely to arrest this one in the first place and Billy Vail would surely want him to question her in depth. So as she got in bed with him, already out of that one-piece summer frock, he just proceeded to question her as deep as he could get it up her warm, wet ring-dang-doo.

Chapter 18

Mother Nature gave her daughters an unfair advantage, allowing them an edge on mere men when it came to whoring, spying and other cold-blooded fornication. But if old Ysabela wasn't enjoying it at all she was one hell of an actress and since variety was the spice of a tumbleweed life he was glad to learn that had she been built any different from that younger Osage gal, Sally Arrowmaker, one of them would have had to be deformed.

Aside from curving different and having softer hide, Ysabela had let her pubic hair grow, and albeit she didn't have as thick a thatch down yonder as the strapping blond Frieda and the hairless Red Robin, sandwiched between the two fuzzy bedmates was an inspiring memory by the time he'd humped Ysabela enough to require a little reverie as they tried for another, dog style.

Pausing for second wind, a smoke and some pillow conversation, now that he knew her right well in the biblical sense, Longarm probed the Indian gal passing for Tex-Mex about her past and she seemed to be willing to talk to a really swell enemy, as described in her Uto-Aztec dialect. It beat all how some Indians could get all mushy about a white man raised Christian who simply followed the Golden Rule and didn't laugh at Indian notions before he tried to understand them.

Ysabela confessed she'd started out as a gal called Sings-Alone, over to Palo Duro Canyon as a member in good standing of the Kwahadi clan. She'd learned Spanish as her first *Saltu* language off friendly Mex traders, the so-called Comancheros, who ran guns to the buffalo-hunting Comanche in exchange for hides and loot from raided Texican settlements. She confessed without shame that she'd sharpened her Spanish up with a Comanchero she'd shacked up with after the bad times of '74.

Bad times for the Comanche, she meant. She said. "That was the autumn your people sent five columns out across the Staked Plains to finish it. Your bear coat, Miles, marched down from Fort Dodge. Three Fingers Macken-zie came at us from Fort Concho to the south. From the west, out of Fort Bascom, the yellow leaf called Price led another column across the Pecos. Eagle chiefs called Buell and Davidson came from Fort Richardson and Fort Sill. Three Fingers Mackenzie had Tonkawa scouts. There was no way to throw him off our trails as all the bands re-treated into the place of the white berry trees the Mexicans named Palo Duro Canyon. It was beautiful there when I was younger. The valley is too broad to call a canyon, with much fat grass for horse, buffalo and elk to graze and nobody else around to bother us. But then Three Fin-gers Mackenzie rode in to bother us. He had big guns on wheels. Anyone trying to stand against their widespread attack was blown to pieces. By the end of the first day the blue sleeves had burned most of our lodges, captured all our winter food and rounded up a thousand ponies. Then they started to shoot them. That is a very ugly way to wage war."

Longarm passed her the cheroot and calmly replied,

"Ain't no pretty way to wage war and our ways work. Long before you noble savages lost your means of transportation at Palo Duro the man who started this house we're in this evening lost his hair to Eyes-All-Over."

She passed back the smoke to protest, "That was a fair fight. As we tried to get away from Three Fingers Mackenzie, later, those other columns rode in from all directions. It was not a battle. It was a buffalo run, with my people the prey they were running down. I got away in the dark by running in a different direction than the rest of my people. After much hungry walking I found some Kiowa who'd escaped with their ponies. We rode by night and hid by day until we fell in with the friendly Mexicans I told you about. They were running for Mexico because your star chief, Sherman, wanted to hang them for trading guns for buffalo hides. Star Chief Sherman fights with eyes of iron and a heart of stone!"

Longarm said, "Heaps of folk in Georgia would agree with you and Sherman, himself, said war was hell. But, like I said, his way works and I'm more interested in you, personal, than the sad tales of Mister Lo. I can see why you decided to pass for Tex-Mex instead of rejoining your defeated nation. Some Texicans have bitter memories of the Shining Times of the Comanche. But that ain't the question before the house."

Pausing to choose his words, he asked, "How come you stayed on here, rising from serving maid to housekeeper after the older Widow Marner hired Shadow Medicine to kill your chief and then he did so, despite your warning?"

She shrugged a bare shoulder against his armpit to ask in a resigned voice, "Where would I have gone? As a Comanche I would be hated anywhere off the reservation and Eyes-All-Over was not my chief. I felt what was in an older woman's heart and once I had sent word to my own people it was out of my hands. The killing made the

157

old woman feel better about her dead husband and to tell the truth I felt . . . proud that a man of my nation, still living free, could get away with murder under the noses of your army and your B.I.A. So I accepted the way things had ended, with her husband and the man who'd killed him both dead. Then, as you saw as soon as you came here with that pale horse and your strong medicine, I allowed myself to learn more English and win more trust until I became the head of this household staff. I hired no more Mexicans as earlier ones moved on. The Widow Consuela has never paid much attention to me and prefers to speak English. But over the years there were times I was certain my stories about my fine old Spanish family had raised some eyebrows."

Longarm soothed, "It ain't considered polite to question folk sporting coats of arms, and my breed is more used to folk who came over from, say, Sweden on the Mayflower. What can you tell me about the more recent death of the old lady's only child at the hands of the same Shadow Medicine, if that's what happened?"

She said, "I think Shadow Medicine must have been the one who shot Courtney up north. Tiny Fulton was there and his description of the killer fits. Courtney was called Cracker because he was loud and crude. But I think Shadow Medicine killed him just for recognizing him. They had naturally met when Shadow Medicine spent some time here the summer of Little Bighorn. Cracker was running the stock operations as Tiny runs them now. They never told me. But I'm sure Cracker knew who'd avenged his father. So he may have been greeting Shadow Medicine in his crude joshing way when he called him his long-lost bastard. I think a hired gun on some other secret mission shot him before he could given anything else away!"

Longarm said, "I suspect you're right. Let's talk about

Frisco and Pud, hired in turn to clean the plow of Shadow Medicine."

She insisted, "I told you. I never heard of either. I don't know who sent them after Shadow Medicine. I don't see how it could be anyone I know."

He asked how come she felt so sure and she eliminated the older widow for him right off. He aimed to check on it, of course, but if she was telling the truth about the older widow having a stroke and winding up in the county hospital as a drooling vegetable she'd sort of paid for her earlier crime and couldn't have hired killers who'd been run out of California after she'd been put out of action.

He asked to hear more about the younger widow, Cracker's Tex-Mex wife, Dulcenia. He had to screw Ysabela some more to get that family secret out of her.

Once he had, it developed that as they lay there conversing with his organ grinder soaking inside her, Ysabela felt sure Miss Dulcenia was up to the same thing with a married banker in town. Ysabela said the copper-haired *sangre azul* or Spanish blue blood seemed to think she was too good for mestizos, or Mexicans of darker complexion. Ysabela answered another question by confiding that the younger Widow Marner seemed to go for rich but crude Anglo bully boys for some reason.

Longarm moved inside her enough to keep it hard as he allowed a naturally stuck-up gal was attracted to men who made her feel scared and shemale. Lots of mean, ugly rich men got on swell with pretty women and it wasn't just their money alone. Some women liked to feel everyone else was scared of the man who ate their pussy.

Moving slow but stead in Ysabela's, Longarm mused, "Try as I might I'm having a tough time picturing our naughty Dulcenia as a grieving widow. After that I don't see how she'd have had time to hire California owlhoot riders, busy with a love affair down here in Texas."

159

Ysabela commenced to thrust her hips languidly as she told him in a suprisingly conversational tone to anybody less experienced, "I don't like her. She thinks she's the Queen of Spain and soon this will all be hers and she may fire me. But I don't think she cared, I think she was glad when we heard her loudmouthed husband had been shot on the way to market with the herd. She's already had to shave between her legs after he brought some crabs home to her. I know that banker she's with tonight was not the first lover she ever had on the side. But I suppose she *could* have gotten in touch with those hired guns by mail, perhaps through some go-between."

Longarm spread her thighs to treat her right with an elbow hooked under either upraised knee as he replied, "I doubt it. I suspect I just eliminated two whole dots from the puzzle and the long trip down this way has been rewarding in other ways, you hot-natured little thing."

She hugged his bare chest down against her and started sobbing up at him in Ho, as the speakers of her widespread dialect defined their common humanity. So even though he only knew a few words of any such lingo he figured it was safe to assume she was really hot and really coming, that time.

He was glad. It allowed him to screw her some more with a clear conscience, knowing they were really pals and that he'd never have to explain all this to his home office.

Some kindly French sage had once observed that no man ever thinks more sanely than he does on a full belly after some good fucking. So next morning, thinking sane, Longarm loped Old Glacier back and all over town to make certain Ysabela hadn't been trying to take unfair advantage of his weak nature. The county hospital was there in Swenson and when he tried to talk to the withered old wreck they wheeled out to the garden for him, he saw

Miss Melony Marner couldn't have hired anybody since her stroke the summer before.

More discreet investigation established that most everyone in town but that banker's wife knew Dulcenia Marner was shacked up with him at the Hotel Brazos. So he rode Old Glacier back to the livery and headed back the way he'd come with those other livery ponies. The only bright spot in an otherwise tedious retracing of his trip down from Hardwater was the rest stop in Rusty Springs with Red Robin.

As they shared *their* second-wind cheroot after some totally novel slap and tickle, Red Robin said he'd caught her just as she'd been about to move on, bless her restless soul and the slow trade in a cattle town as the spring roundup wound down.

Neither asked whether the other had been to bed with anybody else since last they'd cuddled so friendly. That was an unspoken but important part of their friendly relations. But she naturally wanted to know what had brought him back this way, seeing he'd told her the last time he'd laid her that he was bound for Texas in the hopes of making some arrests.

He explained how neither widow down yonder had panned out. When she marveled, "Then there was never any spiteful widow at all!" he blew a thoughtful smoke ring and replied, "I never said that. That French detective Mr. Poe wrote about was right when he allowed a lawman ought to search for the woman if he couldn't see money as the motive. I've been pondering on which inspired all that mad-dog killing up to Hardwater. Frisco and Pud could have been inspired by both. They've been known to kill for money and some men get to killing foolish when inspired by your unfair sex."

Red Robin chuckled knowingly and said she'd noticed that. Then she asked point-blank whether he'd screwed one or both of those Widows Marner, seeing he'd wound up with such friendly feelings for the both of them.

Longarm was surprised and caught off guard by her question, as she'd doubtless planned. But he was able to tell her truthfully with a clear conscience, "I never held hands with either of them. Like I told you, old Miss Melony's been reduced to a spiteful vegetable and I never laid eyes on Miss Dulcenia. She was shacked up with her banker all the time I was there. I eliminated them as dots on my picture puzzle because neither worked for toad squat as likely suspects. Miss Melony lacked the means and Miss Dulcenia lacked the motive. Shadow Medicine added years of enjoyment to her life and once his mother dies she'll wind up with all the property of a man she'd learned to despise. She may or may not have been in on the revenge killing of that Comanche war chief. If the B.I.A. dosen't want to reopen that case it's none of this child's beeswax, and what are you crying about, Red Robin?"

The cuddlesome henna-rinsed bundle in his arms was shaking like jelly aboard a stagecoach as she sobbed, "I'm so ashamed, Custis! You never said a word that time I rode over the Front Range with a good-looking mining man who'd asked me first that evening. So what gave me the right to ask if you'd been swapping spit with widow women down Texas way, as if we had some sort of understanding?"

He said, "We do have an understanding, Red Robin. We each understand that neither one of us is ready to settle down or even lope along the primrose path yoked tight together. So let's not speak of mining men or suspicious widows when there's nobody but us in this feather bed at the moment."

But as he commenced to make love to her some more she sobbed that she was so glad she could tell he hadn't been getting any lately, either. She sobbed, "I'm not in love with you. I won't let myself fall into that pit trap with any man, lest I never get out and end up old before my time like my poor momma! But just the same I can't help feeling grand that you've been true to me, in your own fashion, since you treated me so fine on your way to Texas!"

He felt true to all his lady friends, in his own fashion, which was sheer admiration for the one he was with at the moment. So they screwed like mink, slept late to screw some more and then he had to ride on up to Hardwater to wind all this bullshit up.

Chapter 19

When he rode into Hardwater at dusk as he'd meant to, Longarm left the livery ponies he'd hired in Kanorado with Chester Bedford but told the iron-mustached livery-man he'd be needing to hire a good night rider in an hour or less.

Then he went to the Western Union to see if there were any answers to wires he'd sent earlier to Forts Sill and Smith. There were. So he scanned them as he supped light on a Denver omelet and home fries, lest he feel like shit-ting later at an awkward time.

At the clinic he found Frieda Arnhorst had just gone home for her own supper. The night nurse, flat chested but otherwise not bad, told him they'd sent Marshal Breen home, too. The older lawman was still too weak to ride, but out of danger unless Doc Templar needed to study medicine some more.

So Longarm strode to the nearby Colson home, where he found Tim Colson smoking on his porch swing whilst his woman did the supper dishes inside.

Bracing one leg up on the porch sill, Longarm said, "I could use some help making some arrests, Tim."

The younger lawman rose to his feet and said, "You got it. Just let me get my hat and gun."

As he strapped on his six-gun, telling his worried woman he'd be back when he got back, Longarm lounged in the open doorway. So the kid asked him when they'd be back.

Longarm said, "Nothing is certain but death and taxes, ma'am. But we ain't riding far. It's the paperwork after you make your arrests that can keep a lawman up past his bedtime."

The young deputy's younger wife was a pretty little thing. So as the two of them strode away in the murky light Longarm told Colson, "I need a corporal's squad of eight to cover one homespread on all four sides. You'd know your local posse riders better than me, pard. But you could stay here with your lady once you helped me pick them out and recruit them."

To which Tim Colson replied in a determined tone, "I'm riding with you. Where are we riding and who's homespread are we planning to surround on all sides?"

Longarm said, "The Macropolis place. I wanted to make sure Spyros, the younger brother, would have finished for the day at the saloon. After that it's easier to surround a prairie pig farm after dark than by broad day. Once we have two men covering all the ways out, you and me can ride in to confront both brothers and Miss Alice."

Colson gasped, "Hot damn! What charge are we arresting them fool Greeks on?"

Longarm said, "Aiding and abetting for certain. Mayhaps murder. I still have some dots to connect, so it's sort of complicated and further along, as the song assures, you will, if you just tag along and listen tight, know more about it. I got to work out some of the details with the three of them."

But he did explain in passing as they recruited eight good-old boys for some night riding and got everybody mounted up, how the federal court at the town of Fort Smith outside the older military reservation had confirmed that a Stavros Macropolis had done six months for robbing the safe of the hotel he'd been running, trying to say some mysterious Indian off the nearby Cherokee Reserve had done it. When one of Colson's possemen, a buck-toothed kid called Fred, asked how come any convict had been too stupid to change his name after doing time, Longarm explained, "That wasn't stupid. It was smart. Fort Smith ain't that far and we're always meeting up with old boys who knew us when we were in the army, riding for the Jingle Bob or doing time with them in jail. Macropolis had done his time. He wasn't wanted anywhere when he bought that failed farm off the Widow Norwich and I doubt she'd check the credit of anybody who could pay cash up front. We'll talk about that some more once I've had a word with all concerned."

They rode the short way and fanned out to place two dismounted men with carbines on every side. Then Longarm and Tim Colson rode on in, announced as they did so by the furious barking of pigs and chickens.

Alice Macropolis opened the top leaf of her Dutch door to ask what they wanted at this hour. She said they'd been fixing to turn in for the night. Longarm was too polite to ask whether young Spyros got to join in or only got to watch.

He dismounted and ticked his hat to her as Tim Colson did the same and tethered both their ponies. Then Longarm explained, "You'd better call your menfolk out, Miss Alice. It's a long, sad story and I don't want to have to tell it over and over."

She called to the Brothers Macropolis and stepped out on the veranda with the two lawmen as she asked if anyone had caught those two killers who'd ridden off with their army bays.

He said they hadn't. He wasn't ready to tell her Fort Smith had wired they'd left there on a heavily laden spring wagon, drawn by a pair of handsome Missouri mules.

He waited until the two brothers sharing the same quarters if not *all* the comforts of home had joined him and Colson outside. The lady of the house stood barefoot in her calico Mother Hubbard with her long hair down to her tailbone in back. Both brothers had strapped on six-guns, as gents could be expected to in their own home after supper time. They both seemed anxious to hear what they had to say.

So Longarm said, "Frisco Harrigan and Pud Barker never forced you to swap those livery ponies you turned in for stock of your own. You never had those army bays. You made them up to account for Frisco and Pud not being on the premises."

"Is that so?" demanded Stavros, sticking out his chest a mite to bluster, "If you're so smart, where do you think they are?"

Tim Colson looked more startled than anyone else there when Longarm calmly replied, "On the premises, of course. They never left here. They were riding the Owl-hoot Trail and knew you of old, as an innkeeper inclined to overcharge his customers whether they wanted that much or not. But they knew you were inclined to keep your mouth shut and so they looked you up when they heard you were here, or did you advertise what you had to offer in the way of a luxury hideout here for those who could afford your rates? I grew up on a small holding, Macropolis, so I know how much you can make here, honest, and I doubt you dickered with the Widow Norwich on the price she set. So you took them in when they rode up from the railroad on a buckskin and a cordovan they didn't own. When their money ran low there was no way to sell those livery mounts this close to their home stable. So you told the boys they could earn their keep by performing some chores in their own line of work. You'd been worried for some time about a barkeep and a stable hand who'd stood toe to toe and talked up close to the notorious hired gun of the Comanche persuasion, Shadow Medicine. Shadow Medicine had killed an old chum who'd recognized a mighty sneaky rider waiting in the Boxelder to meet somebody else. That shooting had gone too wild and woolly for anyone else to recall Shadow Medicine as more than a slithery blur. Had Shadow Medicine or either of you boys gunned down that barkeep or that stable hand, the risk would have been as great or greater than keeping Shadow Medicine out here, away from sight. But then, once you had two professional gunslicks at your disposal, it seemed easier to have Frisco and Pud kill those two and only two witnesses off."

"You're full of shit," snarled Macropolis, demanding, "How could we have been so mad-dog dumb, even if we'd wanted Gus Henson and Bobby Arrowmaker dead? Have you forgotten they shot that government brand inspector, another stable hand who hadn't been working there long enough to talk to any mysterious Shadow Medicine and dumb old Marshal Breen, who never laid *eyes* on anybody called Shadow Medicine?"

Longarm nodded and said, "I have not. Such wild shooting must have vexed you considerably. The orders were to gun a barkeep who'd served Shadow Medicine and a stable hand who'd helped the spooky Comanche off and on that blue roan. Nobody had said anything about killing two whole innocent bystanders and putting the town law in the hospital before they finally caught up with Bobby Arrowmaker at the Majestic Hotel. It must have

168

vexed you further when they swore they hadn't shot Marshal Breen *or* the Arrowmaker boy. But let's get back to that blue roan. How did you dispose of *that* awkward pony after Shadow Medicine rode in from town on it?"

Tim Colson yelled, "No! Don't you dare!" as the older brother slapped leather pretty good.

But of course Longarm had been expecting he might and beat him to the draw, easy, to jackknife him over his belt buckle. So the younger brother, Spyros, fell to his knees as Colson threw down on him, to blubber, "Please don't! They made me go along with them! I never wanted to!"

Then somebody else yelled, "Longarm! Behind you!" and another gun roared, a saddle gun, as Longarm whirled to cover Alice Macropolis.

But she was already chasing the derringer she'd been packing to dust, landing limp as spent condom, facedown in the dirt, with her bare toes still on the veranda.

The buck-faced kid they called Fred moved further into the light, holding his smoking Henry at port as he stammered, "Jesus H. Christ, I just shot a woman! I had to shoot her because she was fixing to shoot you, Longarm! You should have been keeping a better eye on her!"

Longarm said, "When you're right, you're right. I was expecting her to play Miss Innocent Squaw, as was her wont on such occasions. She had these other two so pussy-whipped I was afraid I'd never get them to invite her along to their rope dance."

Turning to wave his own smoking weapon at young Spyros, Longarm snapped, "Are you listening to any of this, you pussy-whipped gob of love juice? We're talking about shitting our pants as we hang by the neck until dead, dead, dead! Unless you have something to say that your judge and jury might like to hear."

Spyros whimpered, "I just got here! I hadn't even heard

about that killing last summer until they told those other two to make sure Gus Henson and Bobby Arrowmaker could never give the show away. I work all day at the Boxelder. I wasn't here when they told Frisco to gun the night man there. I'd just gotten off work when he did it!"

Longarm said, "You might have been lucky. Frisco gunned the wrong stable hand and that must have occasioned some testy words indeed. Were you present when they gave those bewildered gunslicks hell for gunning Marshal Breen?"

Spyros whined, "It was after Frisco said he hadn't even gunned the boy they'd ordered him to gun that she shot him with that same double derringer. Then she shot Pud Barker with the second shot, faster than you could blink an eye. Stavros and me buried them under a pigpen, like she told us to. She said nobody would ever look for them there!"

Young Fred, who'd shot the lady under discussion, demanded to be told where in thunder that mean Indian, Shadow Medicine, had been whilst all this had been going on.

Longarm said, "You just shot Shadow Medicine, Fred."

By this time others were drifing into the light, having nobody left there to worry about. Fred snorted, "Surely you jest! She was never no great beauty but surely she was never a *man*?"

Longarm told him to see for himself. Fred gingerly used the muzzle of his Henry to hoist the loose calico skirts of the dead figure at their feet. She had a nice ass. It seemed a shame folk pissed like so when you shot them. But she'd wet down the dust from a shemale crotch, as all could plainly see.

Longarm said, "That was Shadow Medicine's medicine. She could move through any crowd dressed for the occasion, as a beardless assimilated gent or a harmless quill woman, screaming with all the others after a killing in a Comanche camp. I suspect she lured an otherwise suspicious cuss called Eyes-All-Over out for an after-supper stroll through the sticker bushes. Everyone had his killer pictured as a slender rider wearing a Texas hat and a low-slung Colt Lightning. She just sobbed her way off, weeping and wailing in her elk-tooth deerskins like a natural Comanche gal upset by all the commotion. The evening she shot Cracker Marner just for recognizing her she showed how manly she could be with that Colt Lightning. They say Billy the Kid has small hands, too. That may be why he favors that same model .38. But I digress, and Spyros, here, was just fixing to show us which pigpen they buried those other bad boys under. Ain't that right, Spyros?"

The scared and possibly half-innocent Greek allowed he'd do most anything they asked. Longarm hushed the one posseman who just had to make a Greek joke and they commenced to tidy up and take stock as yet more riders, attracted by the gunplay, rode in from all over.

One of them was the Widow Norwich, mounted side-saddle on a handsome thoroughbred and demanding to know why so many dead people seemed to be spread out front of the soddy she'd sold Greek Stavros.

Longarm told her, "We're still working on that, ma'am, and if you'd go home and leave us to some other unpleasant chores I'll be proud to drop by your place and tell you everything I know, later on. You might be able to help me with some loose strings, as a matter of fact."

So she vowed she'd hold him to his promise and rode off in the dark. Longarm got rid of some of the others by asking them to help Spyros Macropolis shift the pigs from that one pen, muck it out, and dig down through soil that reeked of pig wastes.

So Spyros got to dig alone, by lantern light, and he was

a real mess by the time he got anywhere, even though they'd only buried Frisco and Pud a few feet down.

They made him haul the two bodies out, lay them side by side, and slosh the black goo off with buckets of well water to make sure they'd found the right wanted men.

One of the others, experimenting with the long-handled shovel Spyros had leaned against the pigpen rails, called out, "Hey, I suspect there's somebody else buried here. It smells like there is and I feel something squishy with the blade of this shovel!"

Longarm said, "Leave it be. That would be the blue roan nobody has ever been able to account for. Had they been as cute with that horse they'd have been caught sooner. Had they buried all three we might have taken longer to catch them. But sooner or later we'd have caught 'em. It was just a matter of connecting all the dots until they formed one picture or another."

Chapter 20

By the time they'd wrapped up the more tedious paperwork it was far too late to call on an English-speaking
lady. But a promise was a promise and he had a good
excuse. So as soon as he could, Longarm came calling on
Edwina Norwich, certain her snooty butler was going to
tell him to go away, which would let him off the hook.

But, as before, it seemed the steel-rimmed brunette had
been watching from that bay window, albeit with no
lamps lit behind her lace curtains, for she opened the door
again as he came up the stairs, to place a finger to her
mouth and whisper, "Try to keep it down. All my servants
turned in hours ago!"

He'd noticed she had on a kimono of Turkish toweling
and silk slippers with white pom-poms. He whispered
back, "I'll be leaving in the morning with a prisoner in
handcuffs, ma'am. So I figured if I was to keep my promise to drop by it would have to be at this outrageous hour.
We can forget all about it if you're sleepy."

She said, "For heaven's sake, come in and I'll make us
both some hot chocolate. How on earth do you expect me
to go to sleep after that last act of Hamlet at the pig farm
I sold those Greeks?"

He followed her in and up a flight of stairs as he managed not to ask how much she'd asked for the spread she'd only bought with a view to a handsome profit. The now talkative surviving brother had confirmed his suspicions that old Stavros and his women had left Fort Smith well off as well as under a cloud, with more than pigs and chickens in mind.

When they got where she'd been leading him he saw it was another front room with a bay window, a daintier Queen Anne four-poster and a small fireplace, where a copper kettle softly whispered on a bed of expensive cannel coal, imported by rail and freight wagon to suit a rich gal's cultivated tastes.

She sank down to her knees and one hip on a buffalo robe in front of the fireplace, inviting him to do the same as she explained how they could sip hot chocolate and toast marshmallows as they chatted, if he liked.

Longarm took off his hat and coat, then laid his gun belt to one side, nearby, as he allowed he'd noticed the nights were still crisp this far north.

She asked him to explain what on earth had been going on out at that pig farm as she poured boiling water into two big mugs and stirred in sugar, cocoa and cream. So he explained the story started earlier than that and she said they had plenty of time.

He began, "In their Shining Times the Comanche Nation rode high on their stolen Spanish ponies from the Rio Grande to the Arkansas, betwixt the Rockies and hunting grounds disputed by the Osage, the Pawnee and such. In their day, pound for pound, the Comanche killed more folk than any other horse Indians before or since. One of the white men they killed was a prosperous Texas cattle baron, who left a rich as well as grieving widow and the mean little kid they'd produced between them. There was nothing much anybody could do about just another Co-

174

manche killing until after the war, when a Union Army with its hands free and its fighting skills sharpened lean and mean from fighting war chiefs such as Robert E. Lee and Stonewall Jackson, got orders to settle the problems with Mister Lo once and for all. Under the same General Sherman who'd proven war was hell back East, the U.S. Cav kicked the liver and lights out of all the Plains Nations by '77 and if the Apache out under Victorio know what's good for them, they'll stay down in Old Mexico for the foreseeable future. The Comanche, being the meanest, were the first Plains nation the army used artillery on. It seemed to have a wondrously calming effect on them. Most all the bands came in to surrender, a lot of them walking, by the time Custer was having his own troubles with the Lakota Confederacy."

She handed him a mug, asking if it was true General Custer had been a squaw-killing maniac, as some now said.

Longarm replied, "I doubt you could call Lieutenant Colonel Custer a soft-hearted sob sister. But in fairness a lot of ugly stories about him were started by the Indian Ring of the Grant administration. Custer had accused them, justly, of robbing the Indians blind and causing some, not all, of the trouble up in the Black Hills. But I'm sorry I ever mentioned that fight. I was talking about the surrender of the Comanche, when most came in and some held out. One Comanche lady I know avoided reservation life by pretending to be Tex-Mex. Another Comanche lady with a meaner streak put on some clothes and pretended to be a cowboy instead of an Indian. Under the new name of Shadow Medicine, she rode the Owlhoot Trail with outlaws of all complexions. It's not true that there's honor among thieves, but a quick wit and some practice at quick draws got her by until she, as a he, built up a rep as a paid assassin. So it came to pass that as

175

things settled down on the Fort Sill reserve and the family of that long-dead beef baron learned the name of the particular Comanche they had to thank for the killing, they were in the market for a killing of their own and Shadow Medicine was willing, for a handsome price."

She asked how he felt about toasting marshmallows. He said she could go ahead, if she had a mind to, and then he continued, "Spyros Macropolis confirmed what I'd guessed earlier, from what my boss calls the process of eliminating. On the dodge for killing all sorts of folk for money, the prosperous but increasingly hunted Shadow Medicine fell in with Stavros Macropolis, a shady Greek-American dispensing food and shelter along the Owlhoot Trail for riders on the run. Once she'd grown fond enough to disclose her secret to old Stavros they became lovers and she found it duck-soup simple to throw everyone off the track of Shadow Medicine by turning into Alice Macropolis."

"Good heavens! And to think I had business dealings with them!" gasped his kimono-clad hostess, likely unaware her kimono was hanging open some.

Longarm said, "They came up here to start over, pretending to be honest smallholders. They broke even on their casually tended pigs and chickens. Their real profits came from hiding or remounting men on the dodge. So one night, not long after they bought the place off you, Miss Alice had gone down to Kanorado as a she and ridden back as a he aboard a blue roan livery nag she meant to sell a killer on the run aboard a victim's palomino. But whilst drinking alone in the saloon where they were to meet, a jovial bully and former customer recognized the old pal who'd killed his father's killer. So, as Shadow Medicine, she killed him. It was easy. Cracker Marner was said to be good, but he thought he was joshing a friendly Indian."

She said, "I heard about that saloon killing last summer," as she threaded two marshmallows from an open box on one fireplace spit.

Longarm continued, "After the killing she flimflammed Bobby Arrowmaker into thinking she was an Osage, heading off to nowheres on that roan she's meant to swap for a palomino. She knew a few words of Cherokee as well, the same as me. She beelined that blue roan back to the pig farm along beaten paths and after they got rid of it they were out of the horse-trading business and she couldn't meet clients at the Boxelder to show them the way to their chicken-coop hideout. She had to stay Alice Macropolis. They had to send for Greek Stavros's kid brother, an apprentice crook who's been mighty helpful to us with details such as that confused customer who rode in aboard that one palomino. I don't care because that wasn't a federal case. Spyros got a job keeping bar in the Boxelder to show customers the way home to that wayside hideout you sold them."

She protested, "Honest to God, I had no idea, Marshal Long!"

He said, "I'm only a deputy marshal and my friends mostly call me Custis. Spyros told us you were innocent. He says he never killed nobody. The lady of the house was the killer in the family. Albeit she was afraid to kill anybody that close to home. Then Frisco and Pud rode in and she recruited them to do some killing for her. But things went all wrong when Frisco Harrigan turned out too wild and woolly for the cool and calculating Shadow Medicine. He killed the bartender he'd been sent to. Then he killed two innocent bystanders in a row and failed to get Bobby Arrowmaker as she'd told him to."

Longarm's hostess scorched the marshmallows before she saw she had and hauled them out to blow on them, exclaiming, "Do go on!"

He said, "That's about the size of it. Spyros said his sister-in-law and occasional warmer relation gave them pure ned for botching the job and said they could do it right, pay up and ride on or wind up dead. So they wound up dead the evening word came from town that the town law had been seriously wounded whilst Bobby Arrowmaker was getting killed. Spyros says they had an awful row at the supper table, with both outlaw guests denying they'd shot at either target in town and insisting they'd spent the afternoon pretending to be chickens in their secret bunkhouse. Spyros said that Miss Alice proclaimed she'd never been able to abide a lying *Taibo* and then she served them one round each from her double derringer."

"What a dreadful creature!" Edwina exclaimed, deciding those first marshmallows were ruined and scraping them off as Longarm told her, "She almost got me with that same ruse. Fred Dorman saved my bacon and the poor kid's still upset about it. But that's all I can tell you about some dreadful folk indeed who thought they were master criminals and I'd just as soon pass on the marshmallows, ma'am. You made this hot chocolate sweet enough."

She put her messy fireplace spit aside as she frowned thoughtfully and asked, "Just a minute, Custis. You're talking to a woman who reads fine print for a living. You've left something important out. Who shot Marshal Breen and the Arrowmaker boy if it wasn't that horrid Frisco or his partner, Pud?"

Longarm stared into the glowing coals as he soberly replied, "It wasn't important. All the guilty parties are dead or under arrest and we'll say no more about it."

"The devil you say!" she insisted, adding, "How can you leave a lady hanging like this, with such an important part of the story yet to be told?"

He shook his head and said, "Some things are best left

178

untold, ma'am. There's another lady's honor at stake. That's all I can tell you. If I said one more word about it an innocent lady's rep could be ruined. So I don't mean to say another word."

She leaned closer, unaware or not caring he could see she had handsome tits for a woman getting steel rimmed at the temples. She purred, "Oh, you can tell me! I'll never give the secret away."

He said, "I know you won't, ma'am. I think it was old King Henry the Eighth who said two can keep a secret as long as one of them was dead. So not even the lady in question will ever know exactly what happened. Sometimes things are better that way."

She flustered over their mugs as if to make more hot chocolate but took him by the hand, instead, as she softly mused, "My God, I wish other men were as closemouthed about a woman's reputation as you seem to be! I'm still young enough to have certain feelings, but I'd rather die than have people calling me a dirty old widow!"

He quietly suggested, "Aw, you ain't that old. How dirty might you be, Miss Edwina?"

She laughed like hell and sort of moaned, "Oh, God, if only you knew!"

Then she stared at him sort of spooky and rose to tug him to his own feet after her as she decided, "But why shouldn't you know, seeing you've been established as a man who respects a lady's dirty little secrets!"

But of course, once she'd hauled him over to her bed she begged him to be gentle, seeing it had been a spell.

So he tried to start out gentle, but once the ice had been broken old Edwina got to acting like a dirty old widow indeed.

But he was a sport about it and *her* black hair was fine and wavy as well as tinged with steel. Her body, once they'd shucked their duds, was another contrast to anybody he'd been in bed with recent.

But he'd met up with gals built that way in the past and it sure beat all how long, lean gals with big tits, resembling grapefruit halves on ironing boards, all seemed to screw the same sort of hysterical way, bitching and moaning about how you were killing them, all the time they were shoving it up hard to meet every thrust with interest.

She naturally tried all through the night to screw those last few details out of him. But in the end, as it came time for him to go before her servants woke, old Edwina smiled up at him radiantly and thanked him for not only screwing the hell out of her, but assuring her she could trust him to keep it a secret.

So by sunup Longarm had sent his wires, ate his breakfast, settled up at the hotel and the Hardwater lockup, and was on his way with Spyros Macropolis.

As they rode out of town in the early morning light, Longarm told his prisoner they could avoid the curious looks you got traveling across country in handcuffs if the surviving brother would give his word not to get silly.

Spyros gave his word and then never got silly. So Longarm had to carry him all the way back to Denver.

Once there, he handed his prisoner over to the desk sergeant at the Federal House of Detention, left his official report at the office and went up to Capitol Hill to make up for lost time with a softer and somewhat younger widow woman he knew there.

Next morning, at the office, Marshal Billy Vail wouldn't buy his official report as written. Vail blew smoke in his face and snapped, "All right. What am I missing here? If neither of them hired guns shot the town law and finished off that breed kid in the basement of your hotel, who in blue blazes did?"

Longarm cautiously asked, "Off the record, Boss?"

When Vail nodded, Longarm sighed and said, "That was the tragic break that wrecked the clever plans of Shadow Medicine and company. Nobody was after Marshal Breen. Bobby Arrowmaker was trying to shoot *me* from atop Steiner's hardware because he thought I'd been fooling with his sister. You know how some kid brothers are. He winged old Breen instead. Then Amory Steiner fired up through the ceiling to put some busted up rounds of .44-40 in him. He staggered back to the hotel, floundered all over the basement, bleeding to death, and managed to lie to his big sister when she found him dying in that furnace room. He didn't want her to know he'd just tried to murder her lover. When they dug the banged-up rifle rounds out of him they looked to be less powerful .45-Shorts because they'd been slowed to a crawl tearing through a tin ceiling and tarpaper roof. The hundreth of an inch difference ain't easy to measure with the naked eye and the poor kid had *said* he'd been shot with Frisco's Schofield. So why don't we leave it at that?"

Vail said, "I can see why you'd want to. But tell me, did you really make love to his sister?"

Longarm just glared. So Vail never asked again.

JAKE LOGAN
TODAY'S HOTTEST ACTION WESTERN!

LONGARM

Explore the exciting Old West with one of the men who made it wild!

PENGUIN PUTNAM INC.
Online

Your Internet gateway to a virtual environment with
hundreds of entertaining and enlightening books
from Penguin Putnam Inc.

*While you're there, get the latest buzz on
the best authors and books around—*

Tom Clancy, Patricia Cornwell, W.E.B. Griffin,
Nora Roberts, William Gibson, Robin Cook,
Brian Jacques, Catherine Coulter, Stephen King,
Ken Follett, Terry McMillan, and many more!

**Penguin Putnam Online is located at
http://www.penguinputnam.com**

PENGUIN PUTNAM NEWS

Every month you'll get an inside look at our upcom-
ing books and new features on our site. This is an
ongoing effort to provide you with the most
up-to-date information about
our books and authors.

Subscribe to Penguin Putnam News at
http://www.penguinputnam.com/newsletters